# The Case of the Gym Ghost

## Paranormal Cozy Mystery - Ghostly Glenwood Mysteries

B I Skinner

# Contents

# Chapter 1

"Ugh! Look at all these desperate women," Wendy grumbles so loudly, several of them in the packed spin class glare at us.

"Easy there, girl," I tell her, patting her arm, while our friend Juliet steps back in surprise.

"When did *you* become so reasonable?" she asks.

"I'm tired of people complaining that I'm too angry, so I decided it wouldn't hurt to be a little more likable. I've also taken up gardening to relax."

"Bets on how long *that* will last?" Wendy snorts.

"Which?" Juliet laughs.

"Either!" Wendy exclaims while they laugh uproariously.

"You two are hilarious," I tell them.

"We're teasing you," Juliet assures me. "You've changed since you moved here a year ago. You've mellowed."

"It's been a year?" Wendy's mouth falls open.

"Yep." I nod. "It was spring."

"We've done a lot in a year!" Juliet exclaims.

"You don't have to remind me."

"Speaking of doing a lot, did you find Mrs. Abnernathy's safe deposit box key yet?"

"I did," I tell them. "Kind of, anyway. It was as I suspected. The poltergeist had it. Although *had* is the keyword. He flushed it down the toilet."

"Oh, no!" Juliet laughs, before quickly covering her mouth. "I'm sorry, but that's too funny. Can she ask the bank for a new one?"

"Yeah, she told them her grandson flushed it down the toilet."

Even in a paranormal-friendly town like Glenwood Springs, the bank might not take too kindly to a *my poltergeist did it* excuse. "When she told the bank manager it was her three-year-old grandson, he chuckled and said he had two young grandsons himself."

"I bet she was happy you solved the mystery for her, at least," Wendy points out.

"I always appreciate an easy job," I tell her nodding in agreement.

"Easier than solving a murder?"

"Much easier!"

When I first moved to Glenwood Springs, Colorado, from Jupiter, Florida, a year ago, I'd have laughed myself silly if you told me I'd become a Paranormal Private Investigator. At that point, no one else knew I saw dead people. Mind you, I don't just see them; I talk to them.

Since then, I've used my gift as a ghost whisperer to find a stolen tiara and solve two murderers. I know, I have the worst luck. You'd think in a town of only 10,000 people, one wouldn't have that many mysteries to solve, but here I am. Did I mention my bad luck already?

"When you ladies insisted I try this class, you left out the part where it's packed full of adoring fans," I tell them, while scanning the crowded room. The class is overflowing with students who got in line early to snag a spot while others wait at the edges, hoping someone might drop out before it starts. They're all women. Old women. Young women. And every age in between.

"Girl, I told you this class was uber popular! Don't lie!" Wendy insists. My dear, tattooed, pierced, spiky pink-haired friend, who's a potions witch, and the owner of the Looking Glass Bookstore at 6th and Maple, was one of the first people I met after moving here. She has more energy than anyone I know and gives the best hugs. People visit her bookstore just for that. I'm convinced it's because she uses some kind of witchcraft, but she insists it's a plain ol' hug.

"When you said popular, I didn't realize you meant every girl in town would be here jockeying for a spot, though. I wonder if I should sell my spot?" I muse.

"Don't you dare!" Juliet chastises me. "It took us a month to get you here."

"I prefer swimming for exercise," I remind her.

Glenwood Springs is home to the world's largest mineral hot springs. With 3.5 million gallons of water produced daily, tourists have come from all over the world since the late 1800s to swim and soak in its therapeutic water. At 90 degrees in the biggest pool, we swim year-round. Yes, even in the snow.

I swim laps nearly every night, and I don't have to wait in line to do it. I have to exercise often because my other best friend, Juliet, owns the Sol Conceptions Bakery on Grand Avenue. A little short, a little chubby, like every good baker should be, she's the mother of our small group. Always the measured, mature one, she doesn't hesitate to tell it like it is while she peers up at us through her turquoise cat glasses. She often lectures me on losing the chip on my shoulder. She's right. Although I hate to admit it.

I was surprised as a kid when I realized not everyone can see ghosts. My parents assumed I was talking to imaginary friends, but when my friend's grandma died, and we took a casserole to their house, grandma's ghost pulled me aside in the backyard where we were playing and told me she'd hidden money in the attic that she wanted her grandchildren to have. She insisted she couldn't go into the light until they found it.

When I told the adults, they laughed. But when one of them checked it out and actually found the money, they assumed I must have overheard grandma talking about it before she died. But that was when my parents realized I was a rare Spirit Communicator. They didn't mind, but thought it would be dangerous if others knew about it. They worried some would try to take advantage of me while others might be fearful and shun me.

When my parents died, I was only ten years old, so I went into foster care, where I quickly learned to hide my gift. In fact, I hid it from the world until I arrived in Glenwood, and the Red Castle Hotel Bar manager, where I applied for a job, caught me talking to a ghost. He then begged me to use my abilities to communicate with the hotel ghosts to learn what happened to a stolen tiara.

"Uh oh, I sense a fight brewing," Wendy says, elbowing us and pointing at two women next to the spin cycle area.

"He's mine!" one shrieks while the other one pushes her so hard she stumbles backward against a bike, forcing the person who's trying to use it to flail about.

"You witch!" she shouts, while untangling herself from the bike and the hapless person who refuses to give up that same bike.

Oh, and she didn't really say witch...

# Chapter 2

"What is that all about?" I ask, wondering if I actually want to know the answer.

"That's Mia and Erica, who, from what I've overheard in the locker room, are both dating Dillon Watkins," Wendy explains knowingly.

"The instructor?"

"Yes."

"Of this class?"

"Yes," Wendy says.

"Wow."

A crowd of onlookers builds while the women continue to circle each other.

"Shouldn't someone stop this?" I ask.

"Do you want to?" Juliet says.

"Oh no, you couldn't pay me enough to get in the middle of something like that," I assure them.

But when Erica calls Mia a name that one should never use in front of polite company, right before throwing a curse at her, leaving an angry welt on the side of her face, a man from the back of the crowd shouts, "All right, that's it, break it up!"

The man is Sheriff Mack, who, from the way he's dressed, must be working out as well. He has to push several people aside to reach the brawling women. Despite the Sheriff being a large, muscular man, he struggles to separate the pair who have taken to throwing punches like they're in a street fight. Finally, another man who, from the looks of it, is also an instructor, steps in to assist.

When Sheriff Mack catches me watching them, he's surprised at first. A rare smile begins to form until he realizes I'm waiting next to a bike, then he scrunches his face in disappointment like he assumes I'm one of Dillon's groupies. I nearly shout to him that Wendy and Juliet made me come. Wait. Since when do I care what Sheriff Mack thinks of my workout choices?

"Ohhh, boy, did you see the look on Mack's face when he saw Holly?" Wendy exclaims.

"He's so jealous!" Juliet points out while they erupt in a gale of snickers.

"Stop it, you two!" I chastise them.

"Has he asked you out yet?" Wendy presses.

"No, he hasn't asked me out. He's not going to. You guys are so far off base you don't know what you're talking about." I chew them out after watching them exchange knowing glances. They've been insisting for several months that the Sheriff and my boss at the hotel, Gabriel Molina, who's rumored to be a shapeshifter, are interested in me romantically. I think Wendy and Juliet enjoy the drama.

"Hey, how are your new cats?" I ask Wendy.

"Subject changed," she laughs. "But they're doing great. Thanks for asking. Eeyore is still mostly hiding in the backroom while Roo winds her way through the bookshelves, peeking at me occasionally. But Rabbit sprints to greet every customer who walks in the door. They're so dang cute. I love them so much," Wendy sighs contentedly.

"I can't believe you haven't posted them to your Instagram account yet," Juliet says.

"I wanted to give them some time to adjust before they become famous," she explains.

Wendy recently adopted three cats. Yes, three cats at once. Their guardian passed away, but no one in her family wanted them. They actually threatened to set them loose on the street where they'd undoubtedly get injured or sick or end up as some predator's lunch. So Wendy insisted she take all three. Now they're the bookstore mascots. She got them so recently I haven't met them. I'm dying to know what they look like.

"All right ladies, time to work!" the instructor, who I assume is the famous Dillon Watkins, claps his hands, bounding into the room. Besides being absurdly good-looking, his energy and enthusiasm for a grueling workout is contagious. The ladies in the room cheer and wave their hands. I'm so excited, much to Wendy and Juliet's shock, I clap my hands, shouting, "Woo hoo! Let's go!"

"What? I told you I've mellowed," I insist, while they gawk at me.

"How's everybody doing today?" Dillon yells over the din which is instantly met with more boisterous cheering.

"Looks like we have a new girl!" he points out as everyone mounts their bikes, preparing to sweat and huff and puff. Until everyone turns to stare, I don't realize he's talking about me as the new girl. How embarrassing. I give a brief wave before turning ten shades of pink. When I catch the Sheriff watching me again with disdain, I turn pinker. Who knew when I agreed to take this class that there'd be so much drama involved!

We take to our bikes, starting with a warmup. "Happy Birthday, Sylvia!" Dillon says, pointing to a middle-aged woman in the second row who claps while everyone cheers her on. This guy is good. I understand why he's so popular. "For those of you who've asked, my sports drink will be on store shelves as early as next month, so stock up when you can because I promise you it will be wildly popular!" he announces. "You don't want to miss out!"

"He and his business partner invented a sports drink," Juliet explains when I turn to her, confusion clouding my face.

"Really?"

"His best friend and business partner Ivan Moss, a geeky-science-nerd, concocted some sports drink which is supposed to be way better than anything else on the market."

"He's a model turned fitness instructor turned sports drink inventor," Wendy further explains.

"He sells all sorts of stuff on the internet, teeth whitener, vitamin supplements, athletic shoes, you name it. Companies pay him to hawk their product on his social media accounts," Juliet tells me.

"But the sports drink is his invention?"

"Yeah, and from what I understand, it's the real deal. The people who have been testing it insist it will be huge."

"If you ladies can talk like that, you aren't exercising hard enough! Let's take it up a notch so the gals in the third row have to sweat!" Dillon insists good-naturedly while I'm embarrassed again.

He kicks the class into high gear and we all respond with a groan. He's right. It's impossible to carry on a conversation at this speed. Wow, this class is tough!

"You're doing great, ladies!" Dillon cheers. "And here's to my new sports drink!" he says, taking a swig from his personalized bottle, only moments before he stops peddling, clutches his chest, and falls to the ground with a sickening thud. Women in the class gasp and scream, while some pretend they're fainting.

The horrified cyclists stop one by one when they realize what happened, except for one student who is so intent on completing her workout she doesn't notice everyone around her staring at the instructor lying painfully still on the ground. The eerie whir of the lone cyclist pedaling, in contrast to the otherwise stunned silence, stands out. Finally, the person next to her whacks her on the arm, pointing to the front of the room.

"Oh dear," is all she says when she finally pauses her workout.

After a moment of horrified silence, Wendy leaps from her bike, running to assist Dillon, who I'm hoping only fainted due to over-exertion. Or maybe he forgot to eat breakfast. So much for that magical sports drink.

Wendy places her fingers against his neck. "He's dead!" she exclaims.

# Chapter 3

The paramedics arrive in short order, but after several fruitless attempts to revive him, much to our shock and dismay, they declare him dead. None of us knows what to do next. We've peeled off into groups, whispering about what we just experienced.

Sheriff Mack assigns a deputy to keep looky loos away from Dillon's body while we await the Coroner. It's disturbing how many people want to take selfies with him. Bob Quimby, the gym owner, finally covers him with a pile of towels.

I overhear some gym members speaking in hushed tones about how the EMTs are certain it was a heart attack or an aneurysm. Some members cry softly, others weep loudly, still others recall which of his classes were their favorite, while we wonder how someone as fit as Dillon could die from a heart attack.

I'm surprised most of us are still there when the Coroner zips the black body bag closed, placing it on the stretcher before wheeling him out into the bright morning sunlight. I think we felt we had to see the process to the end. It seems awkward, though, to walk away as if it were an ordinary day at the gym. It's weirder still that the weather is so cheerful.

It shouldn't be sunny and pleasant when someone dies. Especially someone so young. It should be much more dramatic, with heavy gray storm clouds, pounding thunder, and brilliant jags of lightning crisscrossing the skies. Instead, it's a beautiful spring day with hints of apple blossom scents and singing birds.

"That was a blast, ladies; let's never do this again," I tell them, patting each on the shoulder.

"Like we could have predicted this!" Wendy complains.

"I think I'll stick to my swimming from now on."

Bob reluctantly announces that the gym is closed for now and would everyone please leave as quickly and quietly as possible? When several grumble about his request, he assures us he'll organize a celebration of life gathering as soon as he can.

He's pale and rather nauseated looking. I feel sorry for him. Being closed for a lengthy time will cost him a lot of money. The negative publicity won't be good either. It's bad enough that one of his employees died. Worse still that he died at the gym in the middle of a class.

Eventually, I climb into my absurdly pink, fully restored Volkswagen Bus to head home. I never would have picked a car like this if I had a choice. But when I arrived in Glenwood driving my beloved Subbie, my otherworldly roommate Clara insisted she could tell from the sounds it made that it was about to die. I didn't believe her, of course.

Only one day and several blocks later, it quit in front of the Red Castle Hotel. But wasn't I surprised to find this obnoxiously bright VW Bus that the home sellers had left behind in the garage. There must be some mistake, I insisted. Why would someone leave behind a car they worked so hard to restore?

They were convinced it was haunted; that's why. They weren't mistaken. Clara, who's otherwise tethered to the property where she died, enjoyed sitting inside the bus while watching them restore it. One day they took it for a test drive, and much to her shock, she realized she was still in the bus as they drove down the road. She was so excited she jumped up and down, accidentally kicking the back of the driver's seat. Naturally, this scared them so much they almost drove off the road.

That was it for them. They'd lived with her haunting their house for years; now, she was haunting their car. Unlike me, they can't see her; but they knew from all the trouble she'd caused, there was at least one spirit sharing their home. Clara loves that they were convinced there were more. Imagine the stories they told their friends! Although maybe they refused to tell anyone for fear they'd be laughed at.

Even I didn't realize there was a ghost living there until the day I moved in. Now I share my home with a 143-year-old ghost and a talking ghost cat. Life in Glenwood Springs has been fascinating.

"How was your workout, dear?" Clara asks, when I walk in the door.

"The instructor died!" I tell her, still in shock.

"Died? Who killed him?"

"No one! They're thinking heart attack."

"Sakes alive! A fitness instructor dying of a heart attack?" she exclaims, pressing her hand to her own heart. "I don't believe it!"

"I know it sounds weird, but it happens."

"What did you kids do then?"

"Mostly just stared in shock. Wendy tried to help as soon as he collapsed, but the moment she touched him, she knew his heart had stopped. She gave him CPR, then the paramedics came, and they worked on him for a while, but it was useless. He was a goner."

"I don't suppose his ghost appeared?" she asks.

"Nope."

"Oh well, this otherworldly life isn't for everyone."

"Maybe not. Do you know if those who go into the light and don't become ghosts realize they have a choice?" I ask.

"I don't." She shakes her head sadly. "I just knew I still had too much to do, so I stuck around."

"It's so tragic. He was so young. I wonder if his family lives in town. Imagine what his parents will say when they find out. They'll be devastated."

"Is this the attractive young gentleman who sells things online?"

"Yeah, how did you know?"

"I have Instagram."

"Of course you do."

"Oh! Look! There's the gym on TV!" Clara says, clapping her luminescent hands and pointing. They must have been watching TV while I was out. She and Mystery have several favorite shows, but this time of day, they would have been watching Golden Girls repeats. "Turn it up!" she insists.

"Popular fitness instructor Dillon Watkins died unexpectedly today during a class at the Glenwood Sport Gym. The Medical Examiner has ruled his death a heart attack," the news reader explains.

"I guess you were right," Clara says.

"I guess I was."

"At least he wasn't murdered, right?" she surmises.

"I suppose. It's still so sad, though."

# Chapter 4

"Am I dressed appropriately?" I ask Juliet on our way into the gym.

"Sure?" she shrugs.

"I know it's a funeral, but at a gym, so..." I trail off. I've never been to a funeral held in a gym, so I decided it was best to go with a pretty but subdued navy dress with white polka dots. Not too cheerful, yet not too somber either. "We weren't supposed to wear our workout gear, were we?"

"Technically, it's a celebration of life, not a funeral," Wendy points out.

"What's the difference?" I ask. We had a full military funeral, complete with honor guard, for my husband Ben after he was killed in combat. I've recently considered burying his ashes at the Linwood Cemetery, where they buried the infamous Doc Holliday and where we also experienced an unfortunate incident with a missing tiara last year. Still, I'm not ready to give up his ashes just yet.

When I moved from Florida, I refused to put his ashes on the moving truck. I belted that obnoxiously ornate urn into the passenger seat of my car for the entire trip. Clara suggested I put them on the fireplace shelf, but I declined. I may not be ready to bury them, but I don't think they need to be displayed, either. Ben would have laughed himself silly at the idea of putting him on the fireplace.

"A celebration of life is less sad?" Wendy suggests.

"A guy in his 20s drops dead from a heart attack. Seems pretty sad no matter what," I point out.

"I don't think what we wear matters," Juliet says, warding off our argument.

I'm relieved to see most people are wearing casual dress clothes rather than gym attire, so I must have chosen right, although a few are wearing their Team Dillon merchandise, which is also appropriate, I suppose. For an entire week the town has been buzzing about nothing but Dillon's death. We're all stunned that someone so young and fit could die from a heart attack. In the middle of a workout class, no less. Juliet, Wendy, and I have gained a certain notoriety from being part of the fateful class.

"Check it out," Juliet says, pointing to the man who helped Sheriff Mack tame the women who were fighting before the last class started. "Is it me, or is he glaring at the Dillon's poster?"

"He so is!" Wendy exclaims.

"The poster *is* massive," I point out.

For someone like Dillon, who appeared to live life to the fullest, the celebration of life gathering accurately matches his personality. Wildly colorful and outrageously scented floral displays clog the entryway so much we have to squeeze through them. An enormous poster, the kind you'd see at the movie theater, featuring a shirtless Dillon lifting weights, sits prominently in the lobby.

"There's our friends from the other day," I point to the women who were fighting before Dillon's ill-fated class. They may be on opposite sides of the room, but their angry energy is big enough to fill the entire space.

"Wicked," Wendy whispers. Mia still has an angry red welt on her cheek, which she unsuccessfully tried to cover with makeup. Wendy explains that ordinary aloe vera won't tame a witch's curse. She'll need another witch for that.

"Do you have something to help that poor girl?" Juliet asks.

"Whatever Erica got her with, she got her good. But I have a few things I can try," she says, heading in Mia's direction.

It's comforting to see the crowd gathered for the celebration of life. A veritable who's who of Glenwood. I didn't know Dillon, but we thought it was appropriate to attend the event since we were in his final class.

"Hey, is that Dillon's business partner?" I ask Juliet, pointing to a man in the corner who's nursing a drink and pouting.

"Yes, that's Ivan," she says.

"He doesn't look happy either. I mean, I know his friend and business partner just died, but he has the same expression as the instructor did when he was staring at the poster."

"You're right. He doesn't look heartbroken; he looks angry," Juliet agrees.

"Dillon said the sports drink would be in the stores soon. I assume they'll still sell it, won't they?"

"Maybe he's upset that Dillon is no longer here to help advertise it?" Juliet suggests.

"But if it's as good as they say, would he need Dillon?"

"Beats me! I don't know how these things work."

"She'll come by the Looking Glass later, where I can get a better idea of what type of curse we're dealing with," Wendy tells us after talking with Mia.

"I'm sure she appreciates the assistance," Juliet tells her.

"You guys will never believe what I heard on the way back," Wendy adds. "One of the women here is pregnant with Dillon's baby!"

"No way! How many girlfriends did this guy have?" I ask.

"I'm not sure it's appropriate to gossip at a man's funeral," Juliet scolds us.

"But it's a celebration of life," I remind her.

Wendy laughs when Juliet glares at me. "Who do you think it is?" she asks, ignoring Juliet's warning, moving full steam ahead with the guesswork.

"What if it's Erica or Mia, and that's why they were fighting?" I suggest.

"I can ask Mia when she's in the bookstore!"

"You two," Juliet responds, shaking her head.

"I'd like to make a toast!" a drunk man says, making us all pause while we watch him sway perilously in front of Dillon's poster.

"Who's that?" I ask.

"That's Theo Barlow. He was Dillon's talent agent."

"Fitness instructors have talent agents now?"

"They do when they're as popular as Dillon Watkins."

"Dillon, you ol' son of a gun," he says, raising his glass and swaying so severely I'm convinced he's about to knock it over until someone moves in, to escort him away.

"To Dillon!" the crowd cheers.

"Somehow, I expected the toast to be profound," I muse.

"Not everyone has a way with words," Juliet says, shrugging.

"Hello, ladies," Gabriel Molina, my boss from the Red Castle Hotel Bar, interrupts us. Between the life insurance from my husband, and my hefty severance package from the company in Florida, where I worked in cyber security, I don't actually have to work.

But I thought being a bartender would be fun and relaxing. Little did I know at the time there are a lot of ghosts at the Red Castle Hotel, which led to my becoming a Paranormal Private Investigator. But I still fill in at the bar occasionally when they need me. I enjoy chatting with tourists and ghosts alike.

"Are you free to work this weekend?" Gabriel asks. "My newest bartender quit without notice, so I'm short until I can hire a new one."

"Sure, I can do that," I tell him.

"You look really nice today," he says. "For a funeral, I mean," he mumbles before turning three shades of red and hurrying away.

"Thanks. I think?" I respond, but I don't think he heard me. "Don't even start!" I scold Wendy and Juliet before they can say anything.

"Who us?" Wendy says turning to Juliet as they try unsuccessfully to control their giggling.

"You ladies enjoy stirring up trouble."

"We aren't stirring up anything. You're the one who has two of the most eligible bachelors in town making goo-goo eyes at you."

"I need some punch. Can I get you anything?" I ask, ignoring what they said.

"I've had plenty already," Wendy insists.

"I'm good," Juliet responds, lifting the glass she's holding.

"Fine. I'll be right back."

I pour myself a glass of punch while pondering what silly, yet well-meaning, friends I have. They're out of their minds if they think all these men are interested in me. They're single. Why don't they date them if they're so intent on matchmaking?

"Excuse me," a man whispers behind me.

"Yes?" I turn to see what he wants when-- "Aaieee!" I scream involuntarily I'm so shocked. I drop my glass, splashing several disgruntled people nearby. The man, or more accurately, the *ghost* of Dillon Watkins, is standing in front of me.

# Chapter 5

"**I**'m so sorry! I didn't mean to frighten you!" Dillon's ghost apologizes. "I know you can see me. I assumed it would be all right to approach you."

"You didn't frighten me; I just didn't expect to see your ghost," I whisper. While I no longer go out of my way to hide the fact I see dead people - considering they're everywhere - I don't exactly advertise it either. Glenwood is full of paranormal activity, so most people think little of it, but I'm not ready to tell them that Dillon's spirit is haunting his own gathering.

"Pretty cool party, huh?" he tells me while Wendy and Juliet rush over to us, using their witchcraft to clean up the spilled punch. Once the sticky mess is gone, and the unwitting victims have forgiven me, the rest of them stop staring and return to socializing. Thankfully, they appear to have written off my sudden scream as an emotional funeral response.

"There's a ghost here, isn't there?" Juliet whispers.

"It's Dillon!" I hiss back.

"No way!" Wendy exclaims.

"We need to talk!" Dillon whispers.

"You don't actually have to whisper," I remind him. "No one else can hear you."

"Oh. Yeah. But it's so awesome you can see me!" he says. "I knew the moment you walked in here that you could. Have you always been able to do this?"

"Uh, well, yes." It's odd to be having this kind of conversation with a ghost. Most spirits I encounter have been that way for quite some time, but are excited to talk to a live human. Dillon seems to think this is interesting. "Let's move over here, though, out of the way," I tell him, making my way to the side of the room, signaling at Juliet and Wendy to follow me.

I don't need everyone to see me talking into thin air. If they knew Dillon's ghost was here, they'd all want in on it, and we'd be here all day. "You two stand here," I insist, moving them in front of me.

"This is so exciting!" Wendy says. "I can't believe he's a ghost."

"What is he saying?" Juliet asks. "Tell us everything."

"Ask him which girl is pregnant!" Wendy insists.

"Wendy!" Juliet scolds.

"What? We might as well take advantage of this."

"You *can* go into the light, you know," I tell him while ignoring Wendy.

"Not yet," he insists.

"Why?"

"I'm not going into the light until you find my killer."

"Your killer? You died from a heart attack!" I whisper a little more loudly than I should.

"Someone killed him?" Wendy asks.

"Someone poisoned me," he insists.

"I'm sorry, but the medical examiner says it was a heart attack."

"How could someone like me have a heart attack?" he persists.

"It happens."

"It's unusual."

"Okay, but not impossible."

"I'm telling you, someone killed me."

"How do you know?"

"Is he still saying someone killed him?" Juliet asks. "How could he be murdered? We watched him die right in front of us. No one was near him."

"Hang on!" I tell her impatiently.

"Okay, fine," Dillon says.

"No, not you, her," I jab my finger at Juliet. This is harder than usual. I admit I often forget to translate for the non-ghost whisperers. I get so involved with talking to the ghosts, I fail to clue everyone else in on our conversation.

"The sports drink in my water bottle tasted funny. I'm telling you, someone poisoned me."

"What's he saying now?" Wendy asks.

"He says someone poisoned him. The drink in his bottle tasted funny."

"He died after he took a big drink from the bottle," Juliet reminds us.

"But the medical examiner didn't detect poison. He said it was a heart attack."

"We could test for poison in the water bottle!" Wendy suggests. "It would be so CSI!" she exclaims, growing more excited by the moment.

"Yes! Do that!" Dillon's ghost says, trying to high-five Wendy, only to be disappointed when she doesn't see his hand in the air. Instead of putting it down, though, he continues holding it aloft.

Is it weird that I feel sorry for the guy? Aside from the whole dying thing, there he is, his opaque hand in the air, waiting for a response. No one should have their high five go unanswered. Not even a ghost.

"He wants you to high-five him, Wendy," I tell her. I can't believe I actually said that.

"Shazaam, that's outstanding," Wendy giggles, high-fiving the air indiscriminately, completely missing Dillon's ghostly hand.

"Eh, close enough." He shrugs, finally putting it down.

"How do we know where his bottle is?" I point out.

We pivot to look at the spin bike area where Dillon died, as if we expect to see the water bottle sitting where he left it. Of course, it isn't there. The pile of towels that Bob used to cover Dillon's body is also gone.

"Obviously, they cleaned afterward," Juliet says with disappointment.

"I don't know why Bob covered me up. It was kind of cool watching people take selfies," Dillon laments.

"Are you serious?" I ask him.

"Nice to know I was just as popular dead as I was alive," he laughs.

"But that rules out the bottle."

"We should ask Bob what he did with it!" Wendy points out.

"Hmmm. I'm still not buying the idea that someone poisoned him. How could the ME miss something as important as that?"

"Maybe he didn't think to test for poison?" Juliet offers.

"Yeah!" Wendy exclaims. "You heard the paramedics talking. They all thought it was a heart attack, too. If the medical examiner assumed Dillon died from natural causes, he might not have bothered to test for something like poison."

"She has a point," Juliet says. "It's not like we found his body next to the dumpster like we did Chaplain Palmer at the Christmas party."

"Please, you have to convince them to do another autopsy. You must demand they test for poison," Dillon begs.

"I can't," I insist.

"Can't or won't?" he asks, with a pout that I suspect has worked quite well on more than one adoring female fan.

"I can't," I explain, pointing to the colorful urn sitting atop a display in the lobby, surrounded by flowers and cards. "You were cremated."

# Chapter 6

"Wow. Way to rain on my parade," Dillon complains.

"I'm sure this is very frustrating for you - the idea that someone as healthy as yourself would suddenly die from a heart attack must seem impossible, but I don't see the Medical Examiner overlooking poison and murder."

"What's he saying now?" Wendy asks.

"He's still convinced someone murdered him."

"You're telling me you won't investigate my murder?" he whines.

"Why don't you cross over? I hear it's quite pleasant."

"How would you know? You only talk to ghosts who *didn't* go into the light. That's how they become ghosts," he reminds me.

"True, but they tell me it's pleasant and welcoming, so I'm assuming that once you cross over, it's the same. Better, don't you think?"

"I didn't say I'll never cross over," he assures me. "But I need you to find out who killed me first."

"You know there's a time limit, right? Eventually, the light will go out, and once it does, you'll be a ghost forever. Is that what you want? Are you willing to take that chance?"

"If you stop wasting time arguing with me and find out who killed me instead, that won't be a problem, will it?"

"What does he want now?" Juliet asks. "You have to keep us updated."

"He's saying he won't go into the light until I figure out who killed him."

"Are they always this stubborn?" Wendy asks.

"No!" I exclaim. "Although this is the first one I've met who asked me to find his killer. Hey, where are you going?" I ask, nearing panic mode when he heads straight for the mammoth floral display sent from his athletic shoe sponsor.

"What do you mean, where's he going?" Wendy asks. "This is so exciting and so frustrating at the same time! I wish we could see him."

"Oh, believe me, you don't," I tell her.

He struggles with the display at first, trying unsuccessfully to push it over. Despite all my experience, I don't know exactly how this works, but I have noticed that the longer a ghost has been a ghost, the stronger they are. It takes practice, according to Clara.

New ghosts can have an especially hard time infiltrating the physical world. It's also far easier for poltergeists than for your ordinary ghosts to do so. But because he's an ordinary spirit *and* new to the other world, Dillon has to strain to push the display over. I'm convinced he doesn't have the strength. Hopefully, he'll wear himself out and give up.

But much to my horror, he works at it long enough and hard enough that eventually, the flowers begin to tilt and rock. After a while, all that rocking draws attention. The more it moves, the quieter everyone gets. No need to explain to Juliet and Wendy what's happening now. They can see it for themselves.

No one else watching understands how this floral display can move on its own, but now people are pointing and whispering to each other. I want to tell him his tantrum won't work on me. Like I haven't dealt with stubborn ghosts before. But if I say that out loud, everyone will know for sure. Which is probably what he wants.

He finally pushes hard enough that the entire arrangement crashes to the ground with a loud bang, sending colored carnations flying every which way. When one lands in a woman's hair, she yelps and throws it to the ground.

Everyone near her backs up like they expect the carnation to take on a life of its own.

"I never liked carnations anyway," Dillon grumbles. "Who sends carnations? What a bunch of cheapskates."

The crowd murmurs with growing intensity after everyone starts talking at once. They may not be able to see or hear Dillon's ghost, but they know something isn't right. Bob rushes over to put the display upright. Only now, it's bent at an unnatural angle and missing large sections of flowers. It looks sad.

"Nothing to see here, folks! No worries! The stand wasn't strong enough to hold the big display!" Bob announces. The word ghost gets mentioned several times among the people watching. "I assure you the gym isn't haunted," he tries to laugh it off as a joke, but it sounds like a garbled plea instead.

Earlier, I overheard some of the staff talking about how staying closed all week cost the gym a lot of money. I know Bob planned to re-open after the ceremony, but if Dillon continues to cause trouble, he may have to postpone. The last thing Bob needs are rumors that his gym is haunted.

But when I think Dillon's done with his tantrum, I'm wrong. He approaches a woman holding a glass of punch and tries to knock it out of her hands. But, he's only strong enough to jiggle it, spilling it onto her skirt. She quickly places the glass on the counter, telling her husband they're leaving. Several others then decide it's time for them to leave as well. No doubt before any other ghostly hijinks occur. Bob's shoulders sag while he sighs loudly. This has been a dreadful week for him.

"How do you like them apples?" Dillon laughs when he casually strolls back to us..

"That's rude!" I tell him.

"Is he back?" Wendy asks. "This is hard to follow."

"*Please* find my killer!" Dillon begs.

I don't appreciate being blackmailed by a ghost, but Bob looks like he's going to cry any moment now.

"All right, let's assume for one moment that you were murdered--"

"--I promise you. I was murdered."

"Okay, fine. Someone murdered you. Who would it be? Who hated you enough to poison you? Although I'm beginning to see you were kind of a spoiled brat, weren't you?"

"Joel Frank was always insanely jealous of my success."

"Who's Joel Frank?"

"He's the instructor we saw glaring at the poster," Juliet explains.

"You saw that too? It was so obvious!" Dillon says.

"We all saw it," I tell him. "You honestly think he was so jealous of your popularity that he would kill you? That's rather drastic."

When he heads toward another display, I throw up my hands. "All right, all right, all right. If you promise to stop haunting the gym, I'll investigate your case for one week. If, after that, I'm still sure you died from natural causes, you agree to never haunt the gym again."

"You promise you'll investigate for reals? Not just pretend because I can't see you after you leave here. Because believe me, I've been trying."

"I promise I will give it my all. But you also have to promise me that if, and that's a big if, I find your killer, you'll still go into the light like you said you would."

"Deal," Dillon agrees.

"What did he say? Did he agree to the deal?" Wendy asks.

"He agreed," I nod. There's a first for everything. Blackmailed by a ghost. Certainly not how I thought a celebration of life was supposed to end. Now we look for a killer. Or make that *alleged* killer. I'm still not sure I believe the guy, or ghost I guess, but he's certainly persistent.

# Chapter 7

"We're seriously solving another murder?" Juliet asks. "Is it me, or is this becoming a pattern?"

"Now that you mention it, we do this a lot, don't we?" Wendy says.

"Maybe," I ponder, "but this is the first time a ghost hired us to find his murderer, right?"

"It's sus," Wendy responds.

"Sus?" I ask. Wendy has the strangest way of talking sometimes.

"She means suspicious," Dillon explains. "And it's not sus. I know what my sports drink is supposed to taste like. Somebody poisoned me."

"Okay, we got it. Let us do our jobs," I tell him.

"Fine," he exclaims testily, wandering off in search of who knows what.

"C'mon ladies, it's not that bad. I told him we'd investigate for a week. If it still points to a heart attack, then we're off the hook. No big deal."

"If we discover it really is murder?" Wendy asks.

"Then we solve the murder--cripes, what's he doing now? Dillon! Dillon!" I try to whisper loud enough for him alone to hear me. It doesn't work because several people nearby stare at me.

"What's wrong? What's he doing?" Juliet asks.

"I think he's about to goose that lady," I explain, pointing in his direction even though they can't see him. Sure enough, he pinches a lady on her backside, who then yells at the innocent man next to her. Good thing she didn't slap him!

"You think that's funny?" she barks at him.

The confused man next to her clearly doesn't, but Dillon does. He's practically rolling on the ground with laughter.

"Get over here!" I hiss, pointing to the spot next to me. People continue to stare, but Dillon reluctantly wanders our way. "If you want me to take this investigation seriously, you must, too!" I chew him out.

"Awww, c'mon, if I'm going to be dead, you should at least let me have a little fun!" he whines.

"Not at the expense of this gym's business!"

"Has anyone told you that you're too grumpy?" he asks.

"Yes!" I shoot back.

"What did he say?" Juliet wonders, raising an eyebrow at me.

"He asked me if anyone has told me I'm too grumpy."

When Juliet and Wendy laugh, Dillon points at them, a grin plastered on his face. "See! I'm right, aren't I?"

"Don't encourage him, you guys. Joel is here, so we should start with him."

"Remember, we still don't know if Dillon was murdered," Juliet reminds me. "It's not like we can just ask him, 'hey, where were you when Dillon died?' and not sound cuckoo."

"We already know where Joel was anyway," Wendy points out. "He was the one who helped Sheriff Mack with the women who were fighting. He was only a few feet away when Dillon died."

"That means he could have easily slipped something into my drink," Dillon points out.

"I would think so," I tell him. Having the alleged victim assist with his own investigation is a little weird. "Do the employees use a different locker room than the members?"

"Yeah, if you want to call it that. It's more like a broom closet turned into a changing area."

"But only the staff has access?" I press.

"We're all given a key. But we lose them a lot, so..."

"So someone other than a staff member might have a key." Why is it so hard to get a straight answer from this guy?

"Yep."

"Ask him if he remembers losing his bottle," Juliet suggests.

"Did you have your bottle with you at all times the day you died?"

"Nah, I leave that thing lying around all the time."

"What's he saying?" Wendy asks, her patience wearing thin.

"He said that not only does the staff often lose their keys to their private changing area, but he also leaves his bottle unattended."

"So anyone could have accessed their locker room or his bottle," Wendy confirms.

"Pretty much."

"Wonderful. So this investigation is more confusing than ever," Juliet moans.

"Ohhh, jinx! Don't say that!" Wendy warns her. "It will only make it worse."

"Joel is over there talking to some guy. Let's wait nearby to grab him as soon as he's done," I suggest. "Although I still don't know what to ask him."

"We make it up as we go along?" Juliet says.

"Tell him you know he killed me," Dillon suggests.

"And then what?" I ask.

"Then the police come and arrest him."

"You obviously don't know Sheriff Mack," I snort.

"I don't, should I?"

"Never mind," I tell him, shaking my head. He'll learn soon enough.

We edge closer to Joel, and the moment he finishes his conversation, we move in so quickly he steps back in surprise. "Hi there?" he asks, bewildered. "Can I help you with something?"

I stare up at him. Even though he's quite tall and good looking, but with longer hair than Dillon, he doesn't have the same presence as Dillon. I'm not surprised he was jealous.

"We were wondering about your relationship with Dillon Watkins," Wendy says.

"My relationship with Dillon? Wait a second, are you reporters?"

"Reporters? No, of course not. We're curious, that's all," I assure him.

"But my relationship with Dillon is a weird thing to ask about."

"We saw you staring at his poster earlier, which made us curious. Were you mad at him?" Juliet asks.

"I don't know that I'd say mad. More like I didn't care for the guy." He lifts a shoulder in indifference.

"Why?" I press.

"This is a bizarre conversation," he tells us, chewing on a fingernail. We stare at him wordlessly, waiting for him to continue. "Okay, I hated the way he flaunted himself. Between all the social media posts, the sponsorships, and then the sports drink. He was all, ohhh look at me! I have a new sponsorship, and I love these shoes from the Shoe King!"

"What's wrong with that? If the Shoe King wanted him to advertise their shoes, why shouldn't he?" Wendy asks.

"Because when the camera was off, he'd mock whoever was sponsoring him. He'd tell us he wouldn't wear those shoes if they paid him. Then he'd laugh and say oh yeah, they *are* paying me. When he was sure no one was filming, he'd dump the shoes in the trash."

"I so did that." Dillon nods, smiling to himself.

"Did his sponsors know?" Juliet asks.

"They didn't care! As long as he was on social media telling people how great they were, that's all they wanted. Everything was a scam. Then his genius friend invents a sports drink, and Dillon talks him into letting him put his name on it and take half the profits."

"Wait, I thought Dillon helped him develop the drink," I point out, staring at Dillon, who is suddenly fascinated with the ground.

"Dillon didn't have two brain cells to rub together except when it came to manipulating people. He convinced Ivan that he would finally become one of the cool kids if Dillon was connected to it." Joel pauses in the middle of his speech like he regrets telling us this. "You know, I'm not sure I should be saying these things to you. I have someplace I have to be," he claims while starting to walk away.

"Okay, wait, one more question," I beg, grabbing at his arm. "Did you have access to Dillon's drinking bottle the day he died?"

"Yeah, sure. In fact, I poisoned it."

# Chapter 8

"**A**h ha! I knew it!" Dillon shouts triumphantly. "I declare a citizen's arrest!"

"What? You can't do that," I insist.

"Why not?"

"Because. You can't."

"Oh yeah? Show me the law that says ghosts can't make citizen's arrests."

"I don't know where the law is, but I'm sure it's somewhere."

"Who are you talking to?" Joel asks.

"It's not important. You just admitted to murder."

"I was joking! Sheez! He had a heart attack. I sometimes joked about how if I killed Dillon maybe they'd give me his sponsorships."

"That's a weird thing to joke about."

"So," he says.

"You're saying you didn't poison him?"

"Of course not! That's the most ridiculous thing I've ever heard," he insists, scanning the room like he's looking for a way out. "Gosh, I just spotted an old friend I want to say hello to, sorry, but I have to go now," he declares, walking away and shaking his head, muttering about how the town is full of the weirdest people.

"That didn't go so well," Dillon says.

"No kidding," I mumble, wondering why Joel got so nervous. I saw the way his eyes darted back and forth, even if I didn't admit it. Why would he joke about poisoning someone? Was it a subconscious confession that slipped out?

"Where to next?" Dillon asks, like he's enjoying this adventure.

"That's for us to decide," I tell him, pointing at Wendy and Juliet.

"It looks like the crowd is thinning out. Why don't we go to the bookstore where we can talk freely," Wendy says, casting a sideways glance in the direction where she assumes Dillon is. "You can meet my new cats!"

"I'm excited to see them!" I tell her.

"Hey! You can't leave me here!" Dillon shouts at us as we make our way to the door.

"We'll be back later," I assure him.

"What am I supposed to do in the meantime?"

"Look for your drinking bottle. We need it if we want to know what you were poisoned with."

"Good idea!"

"Behave yourself too!" I add.

"Awww, bad idea!" he responds.

"Can we trust him?" Juliet asks on our way out.

"No," I tell her. "But it's not like we can move into the gym to babysit him 24/7."

Wendy's bookstore is a small but charming historic house tucked into the corner of 6th and Maple St near the bridge which stretches over the Colorado River. It's one of the first stores I visited when I moved here. And like the first time I saw it, cheerful flowers burst from artfully painted flower boxes on the windowsills, while pastel colored bistro tables entice customers to enjoy a cup of coffee and a book on a lazy Sunday morning. Inside is an espresso machine near several cushy chairs and scattered bean bags. In the winter a crackling fireplace beckons customers to sit and stay awhile.

After using magic to open the front door that's guarded with a safety spell, Wendy coos at the cats "Mommy's home!" There's no need for a traditional security system when you're a witch - even though I once lured a suspect here, claiming the store needed one only so I could interrogate him. Did I mention I didn't tell Wendy beforehand? Boy, was she mad.

I unleash the most embarrassing scream ever when we enter the store because the wackiest creature I've ever seen runs to greet us.

"Shhh! You'll scare my babies!" Wendy scolds me.

"He's...he's...," I almost can't say it out loud, "naked," I whisper. "You didn't tell me you adopted magical cats. They *are* cats, right?"

"They aren't magical, and yes, they're cats. They're ordinary sphinx cats. That's why he's hairless."

"Will it grow back?"

"It didn't fall out; they came like this. There's nothing wrong with them," she says crossly, picking up the one who I'm assuming is must be Rabbit, since she said he's the outgoing one. His purr is so loud I can hear it where I'm standing. I swear he smiles when he rubs his face against Wendy's neck.

"What's so funny?" I ask Juliet, who looks like she can barely contain herself.

"I knew you'd react like this."

"You already knew they're...naked?" I whisper again.

"Stop saying naked," Wendy chastises me.

"I know what a sphinx cat is," Juliet laughs. "You've seen Austin Powers, haven't you?"

"No. Should I?"

"You don't know Mr. Bigglesworth?"

"Errrr, no?"

"Girl, you have to watch it," Juliet insists.

"Here," Wendy says, thrusting the cat in my direction. "Rabbit, meet your Auntie Holly."

"Oh, uh, I don't know if I should." I step back to keep her from handing me the cat.

"You live with a talking ghost cat, but you're afraid of a normal cat?"

"Uhhh, yeah, ghosts, I know. Naked cats, I don't."

"Just hold him," Wendy insists.

Yes, I'm a little afraid of this cat, but I don't want to hurt Wendy's feelings. "Okay, fine," I tell her letting the cat wiggle into my nervous but mostly willing arms.

"Hello, Rabbit," I tell him while he purrs ever louder, rubbing his face against mine. "He's so warm and soft," I tell her in surprise.

"Did you think he'd be cold?" Wendy asks.

"I wasn't sure what he'd be. Does he get cold without hair?"

"He might. I can crochet sweaters for them when it gets colder."

"You crochet?" I ask in surprise.

"No, I'll use magic, silly. You hold him while I check my special book of poisons."

"Look for a poison that gives someone a heart attack," Juliet suggests.

"Aite, will do," Wendy replies while she heads into the back and I continue to hold her vibrating, hairless cat.

What do I do now? He's awfully friendly. Do I pet him? Even without hair? Will he get mad if I put him on the ground? I'm at a loss.

As I ponder what to do next with this odd looking but lovable creature, the bell hanging over the door tinkles when it opens. It's Sheriff Mack. What the heck is he doing here? He stops cold when he sees me holding a cat. For a second I'm convinced he'll turn and walk out.

"What? You've never seen a sphinx cat?" I ask, like I've been around them my entire life.

"Where did you get the naked cat?" he sighs.

"Sheriff Mack!" Juliet exclaims. "Are you here to buy a book, or are you here to see Holly?"

Oh she did not say that!

"I'd like to know what the three of you are up to," he says, refusing to take the bait, much to my relief.

"Hey Sheriff, what a nice surprise. Are you here to see Holly?" Wendy asks, while attempting to hide the book of poisons behind her back.

Ugh. I need new friends.

"I've watched you enough to know when you're up to something. Especially since we recently had an unusual death. Now you're all sneaking around and looking guilty. I have to wonder."

"You might as well tell him, Holly. He knows you can see ghosts, and if it turns out to be murder, we'll have to bring him in on this, anyway."

"Murder?" Sheriff Mack exclaims.

"Gee, thanks, Wendy."

"What is she talking about?" he asks.

"Dillon Watkins' ghost appeared at the celebration of life to tell me he was poisoned."

# Chapter 9

Sheriff Mack stares at us in disbelief while seconds tick by on the clock. We silently return his stare. Why isn't he saying anything? The Sheriff is tall and imposing, exactly like you'd expect the sheriff of a small mountain town to be. His rigid manner, and no nonsense way of dealing with things, can be off putting at times.

His first name is Steve, but I've only used it a few times. Once when I thought he was dying after he saved my life. Wendy and Juliet like to call him Surly Steve behind his back. We've butted heads over a case too many times to count and I've said some not very nice things to him without meaning to. But lately I think he's softened a bit toward me. Or maybe it's me that's softened?

"I'm waiting for you to tell me you're joking, but you're not going to, are you?" he says.

"Nope." I shake my head.

"What did his..." he sighs painfully, "*spirit* tell you?"

"He insists someone put poison in his drinking bottle," I finally admit.

"But the Medical Examiner said it was a heart attack, so that's good enough for me," he insists.

"He's threatening to haunt the gym and cause trouble for Bob if we don't find his killer," Juliet pleads.

"You're the ghost hunters," he says, waving his hand between the three of us. "You figure it out. As far as I'm concerned, there's no crime here," he grunts, turning on his heel, exiting the store as quickly as he came in.

"He's a poet, that one," Juliet adds. "At least now he can't say we're keeping secrets from him, right?"

"Do people think we're ghost hunters, or is he making fun of us?" I ponder out loud.

"Change your mind about the murder?" Wendy asks when the bell chimes again.

"I'm sorry?" Mia says.

"Oops, sorry about that," Wendy responds. "I thought you were the Sheriff."

"Someone was murdered?" Mia asks, concern etching her red, blotchy face, which I swear looks worse than it did a little bit ago when we saw her at the gym. Even with the welts on her face, it's obvious she's a very pretty girl. It's no surprise with her big blue eyes and long, shiny blonde hair why Dillon was interested in her.

"We were joking. Never mind us," Juliet assures her.

Mia's puzzled look says she isn't convinced that murder is something we should joke about, but she doesn't ask any more questions.

"You mentioned you might be able to help me?" she asks Wendy, pointing to the angry welts on her face.

"Oh, girl, you poor thing, let's have a closer look at this," she says, stashing the book of poisons with Juliet while she grabs for the tall yellow stool she keeps behind the counter. "Hop up," she insists, patting it. "She got you pretty good, didn't she?"

"Can you help me?" Mia begs, her voice cracking.

"Sis, if I couldn't help you, I wouldn't have invited you. You sit tight while I see what I have in the back. You're in luck because tonight is a new moon. A sort of cosmic reset if you will. Which means the potion should be most effective for the next three days. You'll use the moon's energy to speed the healing process."

"Thank you," Mia sniffles as Wendy heads to the back.

Juliet crooks her head in Mia's direction while I stare back at her, confused. "Oh!" I exclaim when I realize what she's getting at. Mia and Erica came to blows over Dillon - Mia is a suspect!

"There was a nice turnout at the celebration of life today," I start. I never realized how much easier this is when everyone knows the victim is truly a victim. In that case, I can simply ask the suspects why they hated the dead guy and where were they when he died? Now I'll have to think of more creative ways to question people who have no idea they're suspects.

"Yes, it was," she says sadly.

"Did you--"

"--he told me he loved me!" she interrupts.

"Dillon?" I ask, even though I know it's him. At least I hope it's him, or we have more of a mystery than I realized.

"We were moving in together!" she exclaims, a fat tear sliding down her swollen cheek.

"Really?" Juliet asks.

"Oh, I see; you've heard the rumors about Erica being pregnant, haven't you?" Mia snaps.

"Yes?" I respond, not exactly sure what the best answer is.

"It's not Dillon's baby. He told me so."

"So, he wasn't seeing Erica after all?" Juliet asks.

"He was seeing her. But that was all behind us and we were planning to move forward. He swore it was a mistake, and that she manipulated him. I'm the one he truly loved. I'm the one he wanted to be with. We talked about him moving to Texas with me - where my family lives. He said once the sports drink took off, he could go anywhere. He was going to buy us a huge house. But now he's gone," she wails while the tears come fast and furious.

"Here you go! Oh, dear. What did I miss?" Wendy asks, appearing from the back room with a brilliant ruby red bottle.

"Mia was telling us about her relationship with Dillon," I explain.

"Ohhh, yes. Anyway, here you go." She holds the bottle up to show Mia while uncorking the stopper. It's a short, square shaped bottle decorated with gold filagree. The stopper is crystal colored in the shape of a flame. I must remember to ask her if the potions have to be kept in designer bottles or would any old tupperware container do?

Once she pulls the delicate stopper out though, we back up. The pretty bottle is deceiving because whatever is inside is making us gag. Definitely not like the tea and candle she once gave me to help me get answers to a problem. Those were heavenly. I can't quite place the smell emanating from this bottle. I don't think I want to.

When the putrid scent reaches her nose, Mia weeps again.

"No, no, no, don't worry. As soon as it meets skin, the scent disappears," Wendy assures her.

"So I won't go around smelling like dead fish vomit?" Mia wales.

Dead fish vomit? Not exactly what I was thinking of, but she's not far off.

"Would she rather have those red blotches on her face?" Juliet whispers to me from the side of her mouth.

"Witches honor!" Wendy swears. "Now, you'll need to wait until this evening after the sun has set. If you get impatient and do it earlier, it won't be as effective. You'll only need a few drops. If you use the entire bottle all at once, it's too potent and you'll look worse. A few drops in the palm of your hand then rub it on your cheek in three counterclockwise motions like this," Wendy demonstrates. "Do it on both cheeks. Don't forget to set a strong intention to heal your skin, as well."

"I appreciate this. You've been so nice, and you don't even know me," Mia says after Wendy embraces her.

"I'm sorry for your loss. Whatever problems you might have had with Dillon, I'm sorry he's gone."

"My mom says I should transfer to the University of Texas where I can finish my degree, live at home, and escape all the drama I've been involved in here."

"That's not a bad idea, sugar. I'm sure your mom cares for you a great deal. She wants you to be happy," Juliet tells her, her east Texas accent slipping in, now that she knows she's dealing with a fellow Texan.

"I haven't been able to FaceTime her since I got this!" she jabs her finger at her face.

"Soon, I promise," Wendy says.

"By the way, what are you studying?" Juliet asks.

"Chemistry. Specializing in toxins," Mia tells us.

# Chapter 10

"She's a chemistry major!" I exclaim once Mia leaves. I say it out loud because I still can't believe how coincidental it is.

"Who works with toxins!" Wendy adds.

"Surely she would know how to make poison," I point out. "She'd also have access to supplies in the college laboratory. How perfect is that?"

"Maybe a little too perfect?" Juliet says.

"She has motive too," I plow ahead, ignoring what Juliet said. "Dillon cheated on her with at least one other girl--"

"--you think there's more?" Wendy interrupts.

"It wouldn't surprise me."

"But she said they were past it," Juliet reminds us.

"Please. Like we've never had a suspect who lied," I respond with a roll of my eyes. "We don't know for sure who fathered the baby either."

"Let's check out the poison book to see what she might have used," Wendy says. "It has to be something that looks like a heart attack."

"But undetectable?" Juliet asks.

"They didn't test his blood for poison because they were convinced he died from natural causes," I remind her. "They said heart attack, then cremated him. So it may not have to be undetectable."

"Oh, that's right," Juliet says.

"We need to find the bottle," Wendy murmurs while turning the pages of the thick, leather bound tome.

"What if we find it, but after this much time has passed, they can't detect poison?"

"Anything potent enough to kill someone can't simply disappear, right?" I ask. "Assuming we find the bottle, how will we convince them to test it, anyway?"

"You can sweet talk the Sheriff into it," Wendy says, batting her eyes at me.

I groan and point to the book of poisons to remind them what we're supposed to be doing. These two need to get a life and stop obsessing over mine.

"Oh! Here's a good one!" Wendy says, pointing to a picture of innocent-looking, vibrant purple flowers shaped like tiny bells. "Foxglove," she tells us.

"I've seen those in the park!" Juliet exclaims. "They're poisonous?"

"They used it to poison James Bond in one of his movies," Wendy tells us excitedly.

"You can put it in a drink?" I ask.

"That's what they did in the movie."

"That's a movie, though. We're talking about real life here," I remind them.

"Would it make a person's drink taste different?" Juliet asks.

"Beats me. It doesn't say."

"So, Dillon may have been poisoned with a flower, anyone might find in the park. What else have you got?" I press.

"It says chemotherapy drugs can cause a heart attack."

"Those would be hard to come by, don't you think?" I point out.

"Harder than a common garden flower, yes."

"Keep going."

"Ohhh, what about strychnine?"

"Can you put it in a drink?" Juliet asks.

"According to this, yes."

"That definitely can't be easy to find."

"I wouldn't think so."

"Even though we're unsure of the toxins Mia has access to, we should assume, at the very least, she knows how to use them," Wendy suggests.

"We should definitely follow up on it," Juliet insists.

"Uh oh, I have to go; Gabe needs me to work tonight," I tell them after getting a text from my boss at the hotel. "I should go home and change."

"Have fun with that!" Juliet says coyly.

"Why do you guys keep doing that? You're single too. *You* should go out with one of them. Or both! A double date!"

"But they aren't flirting with us!" Wendy points out.

"Whatever. I still say you're making all of this up. Let me know if you learn anything new from your poison book," I tell them as I walk out the door, grateful for an excuse to escape their suggestions that anyone, much less the Sheriff or my boss, are interested in me.

"Hey everyone, I'm home!" I call out to an empty kitchen. Where's Clara and Mystery? Normally they appear out of thin air, hoping to startle me when I walk in the door.

It worked for about the first hundred times. Now I'm prepared. "Hello?"

"We're in here!" Clara says from the living room

"You sure watch a lot of TV," I point out when I find them glued to the television.

"They're running a Monk marathon on the Cozi channel," Mystery explains, not bothering to look up when I walk into the room. Yes, the cat talks. The first time I realized it I had to sit down.

It was shocking enough to learn that a ghost cat lived in the house with Clara, but to discover she talked was possibly the biggest surprise I'd ever received. Like Clara, Mystery also can ride in the VW and often pesters me to stop at a coffee shop for a catpuccino.

"How was the service, dear?" Clara asks, also refusing to look away from the television. They must have seen every episode of Monk numerous times, yet here they are, unwilling to miss a moment.

"There was a good turnout, lots of people. Oh, and Dillon's ghost talked to me."

That got their attention.

"Who's Dillon?" Mystery asks.

"He's the young man who died of a heart attack!" Clara scolds her.

"Oh yeah," she meows, returning her attention to the TV.

"Did he have anything interesting to say?" Clara asks.

"He says he was murdered."

"What?" they exclaim in stereo. It turns out real-life mysteries are more interesting than television ones.

"He says someone put poison in his drink bottle. He drank it, thought it tasted weird, and next thing he realized, he was a ghost."

"Someone poisoned his water?"

"Technically, it was his sports drink."

"What does Sheriff Mack think about this?" Clara gushes. She has a thing for him which she makes no effort to hide.

"He said the ME insists it was a heart attack, and he believes him over a ghost, so he wasn't interested in anything we had to say. He actually turned around and left afterward he was so disturbed."

"What do *you* think?" Clara asks. "Was he poisoned?"

"I'm not sure what to think at this point. I already talked to another fitness instructor who was jealous of him. He also has at least two women at the gym fighting over him. One of which may or may not be pregnant with his kid."

"Did you talk to either of them?" Mystery asks.

"We talked to the one who isn't pregnant. She insists the baby doesn't belong to Dillon. But she's also a chemistry major, so she knows her poisons."

"Can they test whatever was in the bottle?" Mystery asks. Yes, it's an unusual question for a cat to ask, but they do see a lot of mysteries on television.

"That's the problem. The bottle is missing."

"I saw a show last year where the wife poisoned her husband through his eye drops," Clara tells me.

"Was it a murder mystery show or the real thing?"

"It was real! It was on the news. The coroner said the husband had a heart attack, but his family was suspicious, so they demanded a blood test, and sure enough, they found poison! You must insist on a blood test."

"We can't," I sigh. "He's already been cremated."

"That's a shame. Hey, do you want to watch Monk with us?"

"I can't. Gabe asked me to fill in tonight, so I have to get ready."

"Maybe a ghost in the hotel has heard something useful," Clara points out.

"That's what I'm hoping." The ghosts in the hotel operate as a well-functioning gossip machine. There's always at least one guest in the hotel bar spilling his guts, and a ghost who overhears it.

"We'll keep watching TV, and maybe we can find a clue," Mystery tells me dismissively.

"Yes, you do that," I tell her.

While I'm combing through my closet for my favorite t-shirt, because there's no way I'm wearing a dress to tend bar, my phone buzzes with a text from Wendy.

**My cousin's dentist's next-door neighbor is a mortician. He said while it's a long shot, we might be able to test the cremains for poison.**

Yes!

**I'll go to the gym for the ashes right now!** I text back.

# Chapter 11

This is the break I've been hoping for! We take Dillon's ashes for testing to solve the mystery. No poison? No more mystery. He can go into the light, leaving the gym in peace. Poison? We determine what type it is, then we find the killer. Dillon still goes into the light, finding whatever peace he needs on the other side.

Either way, it's a win. Although, maybe not so much for Dillon, considering he's dead. But at least it gives him answers. Better for the gym, too. The Glenwood Sports Gym isn't one of those big corporate places. It's a small, neighborhood facility which Bob has owned for years. It pains me to see his business harmed by something completely out of his control. Assuming he didn't poison Dillon, of course. But why would he? Dillon's popularity was good for business.

By the time I arrive, there's only one car left in the parking lot if you don't count the mail truck pulling away from the entrance. Good. This way, I don't have to make a scene in front of a crowd about why I need Dillon's ashes. I'm not sure what I'll do once I have them though.

Wendy might be right. Perhaps I could sweet-talk Sheriff Mack into testing the ashes. He may be gruff, but he's fair. I bet flirting won't be necessary. I'll simply appeal to his logic, convincing him he must test the cremains for toxic substances.

If Dillon was poisoned, it means a killer is on the loose in Glenwood Springs, so it only makes sense we go after whoever it is. The Sheriff will surely see that justice is at stake. That should appeal to him more than me telling him how handsome he is.

After parking directly in front of the gym, I skip up the stairs to the entrance. This is all coming together and I feel so much better. But when I pull on the door, it's locked. Phooey.

"Hello!" I call out. "Hello! Bob! Are you in there?" I shout, knocking. This is urgent and I don't want to be late for work. Wait! Yes! He's behind the counter. "Excuse me!" I shout, knocking again.

He looks up, startled by all the banging and shouting, but I'm relieved when, instead of dismissing me, he comes to the door. "Can I help you? We're closed right now, but we'll be open first thing tomorrow."

"Hi, I'm Holly Daniel. I'm a Paranormal Private Investigator. This sounds weird, but please bear with me. I need to borrow Dillon Watkins' ashes. It's official business." I'm hoping by throwing in the word official it will make me appear more...well...official.

"I can't do that," he tells me.

"I know it sounds ludicrous, but it's very important I get them." I was secretly hoping he'd hand them over with no questions asked, but why would he? If it helps, I'm willing to tell him about Dillon's ghost, but I doubt he'll believe me. I should have brought Sheriff Mack along. Except he probably would have refused anyway.

"I mean, I really *can't*," he insists. "The mailman took them right before you showed up. They're on their way to his parents' house in Wyoming."

Of course, it's never as easy as I hoped. But, considering the mail truck just left, I'll try to catch him.

"No problem! Thank you!" I tell him, sprinting for the street. If he had other stops nearby, he'll be easy to find. I won't even be late for work. But now, there's no sign of the truck. Poor Bob still stands in the doorway, completely puzzled about the wacky woman demanding cremains.

I'll never find the truck on foot, but I have a few minutes to spare. Maybe I can track him down in the VW. But after driving in circles for several minutes, I realize it's fruitless.

He's nowhere to be found. If I didn't have to be at the bar, I could go to the post office to ask, but since I promised Gabe I'd fill in tonight I don't want to disappoint him. Perhaps I can hit the post office first thing tomorrow?

"Hey Holly, you okay? I was worried," Gabe asks when I scramble into the Red Castle Hotel, out of breath and frantic.

"Yeah, sorry I'm a little late. I was trying to chase down a mail truck, but it didn't work."

"Did you have a package to mail? You can go directly to the post office you know."

"I didn't have a package. I was trying to get one back."

"So, you accidentally mailed something? You sure are confusing at times."

"No, it's just..." What do I say next? I'm speechless for the moment, wondering how much I should tell him.

"Does this have anything to do with the ghost at the gym?" he finally asks breaking an uncomfortable silence.

"How did you know?"

"It looked like you were talking to an imaginary friend."

"That obvious, huh?" I laugh a little because it reminds me of my parents.

"Only to those of us who know you." He smiles.

"I might as well tell you, too," I sigh heavily. "Dillon Watkins' ghost told me he was murdered."

"Wow! Does this happen a lot?"

"Thankfully, no."

"Hang on a sec. How was he murdered? I thought they said heart attack?"

"He swears his sports drink tasted funny, so he thinks it was poison. I watched him take a swig from the bottle and in moments, he fell off the bike and died."

"You were in his last class? Did you go to his classes a lot?" he asks with what sounds like a touch of jealousy. Great. Now I'm sounding like Wendy and Juliet.

"It was my first one. Juliet and Wendy insisted I try it because they've enjoyed the classes so much."

"Your first class, and the instructor dies in front of you. Can I ask you how it works? I mean, does his spirit hop out of his body and start talking to you or what? I'm sorry, is that a dumb question?"

"No." I smile at him. "He didn't pop out of his body. I only realized that he didn't cross over until the celebration of life today when he approached me to tell me he was poisoned."

"What happens next?"

"I told Sheriff Mack about it, but he doesn't believe me."

"Do *you* think Dillon was murdered?" he asks.

Why must everyone ask me that? "Honestly, I don't know what to think at this point."

"Who would want to kill the guy? I thought he was super popular," Gabe points out.

"So far, we have another instructor at the gym who's jealous of him and one of the women he was involved with."

Gabe nods. "Yeahhh, I heard he was a player."

"Right before he died, two women got into a fight over him, so I still need to talk to the other one for sure. Rumor has it she's pregnant."

"With his kid?" Gabe gasps.

"Supposedly not, but who knows?"

"Hi, Holly! I was hoping you were working tonight!" Fiona, one of my most reliable ghost witnesses, says, popping her head through the wall to greet me. I learned the hard way when Fiona talks, I better pay attention.

"Hi, Fiona, what's up?" I ask. "By the way, Fiona is here," I tell Gabe.

"Yes, I gathered that," he laughs.

"Dillon's Watkins talent agent is in the bar," she says, beckoning me to follow her. "He says he killed Dillon."

# Chapter 12

"**I**'m needed in the bar!" I exclaim.

"What did she say?" Gabe asks after me when I dash from the lobby.

"I'll fill you in later!"

Theo Barlow, Dillon's talent manager, a tall, too-thin man, with rumpled sandy brown hair, perches precariously on a stool at the bar. I hope he isn't too drunk to talk to me. He was already drunk at the celebration of life wasn't he? Uh oh. Please tell me he didn't drive here.

"Good evening Theo! Can I interest you in a glass of water?"

"Good evening, miss! Jeepers, am I drunk, or do you have purple eyes?" he asks, peering at me with a bleary gaze.

"I do. Well, technically, they're lavender."

"They're so pretty!"

"Thank you. Now, how about some water?" I insist, pouring a large glass for him. As a child, the kids bullied me over my lavender eyes and my imaginary friends. I never admitted I was talking to ghosts because I rightly assumed imaginary friends would be far less creepy. Weird, sure, but not as creepy.

Although *I* never thought talking to ghosts was creepy because I'd always done it. But when I realized it wasn't safe to admit I talked to dead people, I ignored the ghosts. Or at least I tried to. They can be stubborn. Once, a ghost threw oranges at me in the grocery store when I refused to acknowledge him, which brought the entire display crashing to the ground. I ran from the store before they blamed me.

But sometimes, I was lonely and wanted someone to talk to. Inevitably, a classmate would catch me and tell the others I was talking to imaginary friends again. I never envisioned when I grew up, people would find my eyes fascinating and, for the most part, not care that I talked to ghosts.

"Did you drive yourself here, hon?" Now I sound like Juliet. Next thing you know, I'll be saying *well, aren't you precious.*

"I don't know how I got here," he slurs.

Uh oh. I hesitate to ask for his keys because experience tells me he won't be happy about it. I'll have Gabe do it because I obviously can't let him drive away. They usually respond better when a man requests their keys anyway. But as I pick up the phone on the bar to call Gabe in his office, Antonio, the ghost, appears. "He took a cab. I saw him when he arrived."

"That's a relief! Thanks for the heads up," I tell him. As a kid, I may have found my gift cumbersome. But as an adult, it comes in handy!

"You were at the celebration of life earlier today," I tell Theo. I'm not sure how helpful interrogating a drunk suspect will be, but I should at least try while he's sitting here.

"Can I tell you a secret?" he asks.

"Sure, why not?"

"Dillon Watkins was about to fire me, so I killed him."

"You don't say." What was in the punch at the gym that is making people confess to murder. "How exactly did you kill him?"

"I, uh, I, well, I, I forget!"

"You forget how you killed him?"

"Killed who?"

We could be here all night.

"Dillon. You told me seconds ago that you killed him." Fiona nods in agreement. Imagine if he knew a ghost was next to him, listening to him confess to murder.

"Who's Dillon?"

I should have known.

"Dillon Watkins is your client. He *was* your client any-way. At the celebration of life, you called him a son of a gun, and just now, you said you killed him."

"Oh yeah! But did I kill him, or did I only think about killing him?"

"I don't know, sir. Here, drink your water."

"But I didn't order water! I ordered a martini!"

"It's not actually water. It's a large martini," I lie.

"Oh, good!" he exclaims, chugging the glass in seconds. "Another large martini barkeep!" he shouts, plopping his glass onto the bar top with a resounding smack.

"Coming right up!" I tell him, serving him a second glass of water.

"Everything all right in here?" Gabe asks, poking his head into the bar area.

"All good. I'm handing out extra large martinis tonight. On the house!"

"Yeah!" Theo shouts, thrusting his glass in the air.

"Martinis are free?" a large man sitting on the other side of the bar asks.

"Not for you," I shake my head.

"Only for me!" Theo says, giggling.

Gabe nods when he realizes what I'm doing. "Do you need me to take someone's car keys?" he asks, approaching the bar.

"We're good. He came in a taxi. I'm trying to rehydrate him."

"Is this someone you know? Is this why Fiona came to get you?" Gabe whispers loudly.

"I don't really know him, but he was at the celebration of life. He's the one who toasted Dillon's poster with a 'you ol' son of a gun.'"

"Oh yeah! It's him, isn't it? He might have been toasting him, but it wasn't friendly, was it? How did he know Dillon?"

"He's his talent agent."

"But he's a fitness instructor."

"Apparently, they have talent agents these days."

"Huh. So he's upset Dillon died, I assume?" Gabe asked.

"He says he killed him."

"He what?"

Gabe and I continue discussing this in front of Theo only because he isn't paying a bit of attention to us. He's too busy playing with the sugar packets that *were* neatly stacked in their ceramic holder.

"He claims Dillon was getting ready to dump him, so he killed him," I explain.

"He claims? But is it true? I mean that Dillon was dumping him? It would give him motive, wouldn't it?"

"If true, it would definitely give him motive. Although in this drunken state, we obviously can't take him seriously. I'll follow up with Dillon about it, though. Remember he could have motive, but he'd have to know what kind of poison would cause a heart attack."

"I don't suppose you have the bottle in question? That would be too easy, right?"

"Hey! You're catching on!" I tell him, playfully hitting him on the arm. "It's never as easy as I hoped. No, I don't have the bottle, but I would love to get it."

"Hang on. Does this have anything to do with why you were chasing the mail truck earlier?"

"Ah, yes, Bob shipped Dillon's cremains to his parents in Wyoming. I was chasing the mail truck, hoping to get them back."

"How will the ashes help?"

"We can try to test them for any poison remnants."

"I have a friend who works in the post office. Want me to call him to see if he can do anything?" he offers.

"That would be amazing."

"I can't guarantee it, but I'll at least ask."

"I'll take anything at this point."

"Hey, hey you," Theo says, jabbing his finger at Gabe. "Doesn't she have the prettiest purple eyes?" he nods in my direction.

"Yes, she does," Gabe says.

"All right, time to put you in a cab and get you home, okay?" I insist before he embarrasses me any further.

"Hey, do you know Ivan Moss? I think he killed Dillon."

# Chapter 13

While wiping down the bar at the end of the night, I mull over the fact I now have at least three suspects for a murder, which may not actually be a murder. How bizarre is it that someone who supposedly died from natural causes has several people claiming they either killed him or know who did? I'm even more perplexed when Sheriff Mack shows up right before closing.

"Good evening Sheriff."

"Ms. Daniel," he grunts, nodding at me. For a moment, I wonder why he still calls me as Ms. Daniel. But I still call him Sheriff, so  it's only fair. For me, it's like Sheriff is his name.

"I've been thinking about what you told me earlier," he says, pausing like he hasn't quite decided what he intends to say.

"About Dillon Watkins being poisoned?"

"Despite my better judgment, I've been looking into it."

"Have you found anything?" This is exciting! He wouldn't come all the way over here if he didn't know anything, would he?

"The medical examiner stands by his ruling of an unexpected heart attack. Everything showed it was death by natural causes, so he didn't see the need to test Watkins' blood for toxins."

"Yet, you're here."

"I am," he sighs loudly. "You said Dillon's ghost told you he was murdered."

"I did."

"And?" he presses impatiently.

"And what?"

"As much as I hate to admit this, you usually have a specific reason for making your arguments. They aren't always *good* reasons, but I've never known you to just make these things up, so here I am. Following up."

"Why, Sheriff Mack. You flatter me."

"Don't expect it to become a habit."

"Fair enough."

"What exactly did this Dillon, uh, his ghost, tell you? Was he threatened? Has someone tried to kill him in the past? Is he looking for attention? What's going on here?" he quizzes me.

"He said the sports drink in his bottle - which he helped invent, by the way - tasted funny. Then he was a ghost."

"That's it?"

"It was at first, but after I started investigating, weird things happened. Dillon said one of the other instructors - Joel Frank - was jealous of him. When we talked to Joel at the ceremony, he joked about killing him."

"He joked?"

I nod.

"Kind of a weird thing to joke about after someone dies."

"I thought so too. In fact, he didn't just say he killed him, he specifically said he poisoned him. When I pressed him on it, he got nervous, insisted he was only joking, then hurried away."

"That is suspicious," Sheriff Mack growls.

"It gets better. Tonight when I arrived at the bar, Fiona, one of my ghost informants, said Theo Barlow was here, insisting *he* killed Dillon."

"Now you're pulling my leg. You have informants?"

"I do. I'm sure *you* have informants." I respond haughtily.

"I'm law enforcement; I'm supposed to have informants. Now don't tell me he confessed to poisoning him, too."

"No, he said he killed him but didn't give specifics, even when I asked him. But he was super drunk, so I kind of dismissed it. Yet just as I was getting ready to send him home in a taxi, he claimed Ivan Moss, Daniel's friend and business partner, killed him."

"You're telling me in one day of investigating, two people confessed to killing a guy who died from a heart attack?"

"That's exactly what I'm telling you."

"Did Theo say why he thinks Ivan killed him?"

"No, he threw up in a potted plant in the lobby after that, so I sent him home."

"My life was easy before you moved here, you know that?" he says.

"Are you saying you find me exciting?" I ask.

"I don't know if I'd call it that. Exasperating. Draining. Exhausting. Those are better words."

"So you're saying I've grown on you?"

"Is there anyone else on your list of suspects?" he sighs. When I pause, he rolls his eyes at me in exasperation. "You might as well tell me now. You know I'll eventually find out. This way, I might be able to help you."

"You believe me?" I ask in surprise.

"I didn't say that, and you know it."

"It looks like Dillon was involved with at least two women."

"Oh, boy!" he exclaims before burying his head in his hands.

"You got it."

"Let me guess. They were the two women who were fighting in the gym before he died."

"Yes! The fight you broke up."

"You said there were more, though."

"I don't know for certain if there were more, but I bet there were. He was quite popular."

"Okay, for now, let's focus on the two who were fighting."

"Erica, who they tell me is pregnant, possibly with Dillon's baby, cursed Mia with a rash on her cheek while they were fighting. Wendy offered to give her a potion to cure it, so she stopped by the bookstore, and we talked to her."

"Don't tell me she confessed to killing him."

"No, she insisted they were in love and moving to Texas together," I tell him.

"You don't believe her?"

"I suspect it was only wishful thinking on her part."

"That doesn't mean she killed him," he points out.

"She's a chemistry major who specializes in toxins."

"She would know how to make poison."

"I would think so."

"She may have a lab at the university."

"See! Now we're starting to think alike!"

"Oh, dear. What about this Erica person? Is she really pregnant?"

"I think so."

"But is it Dillon's baby?"

"Mia says it isn't because Dillon says it isn't."

"Do you believe either of them?"

"Not really," I shake my head.

"Erica didn't confess to killing Dillon, did she? And why is this sounding like a telenovela than real life?"

I shrug. "I haven't talked to her yet."

"Why do things get so complicated when you're around?"

"I don't know. Hey, do you have any pull at the post office?"

"The post office isn't my jurisdiction. It's federal."

"I know, but Gabe said *he* has a friend who works there. He's checking with him. I thought maybe you did too."

"Oh, does he now? But what does the post office have to do with a fitness trainer's secret murder?"

Did he bristle when I mentioned Gabe's name? That's it. I'm spending too much time with Juliet and Wendy.

"They have his ashes."

"Why did I know you'd say something bizarre like that?" He sighs, rubbing his fingers against his temples.

"The ashes are being shipped to his parents in Wyoming. But I'm told there's a possibility we can test them for poison."

"Can you actually do that? It seems unlikely," he says skeptically.

"I know, but Wendy's cousin's dentist's next-door neighbor is a mortician and he says it's possible."

"Wendy's cousin's dentist," the Sheriff scratches his head, "never mind. I don't suppose you know where this allegedly poisoned bottle of sports drink is?"

"That's the other thing we need. If I can find the bottle, could you send it to the lab for testing?"

"Those tests aren't free, you know."

"I know, but what if Dillon really was poisoned? He was a young, healthy athlete. The idea he dropped dead from a heart attack is hard to wrap my head around. I know it's possible, but it doesn't make it likely, right? If he was poisoned, it means there's a murderer running loose in Glenwood. You wouldn't want them to get away with it, would you? As a man of the law, I mean."

"Clever tactic. Using logic and justice to appeal to me."

"But did it work?"

"I'll think about it."

Ha! I've so got him.

# Chapter 14

After learning Erica is a hair stylist at the Glenwood Glow & Go, I call to see if she has an opening today. I know this is the best way to get her to confide in me.

As a hair stylist, surely she would know about chemicals, wouldn't she? Enough to poison someone, though? Probably not in the same way Mia would. Even so, she's around chemicals every day, so she must know more than the average person. Anyway! I'm about to find out.

This will also give me a chance to press her on her baby's daddy. We all saw how angry she was when fighting over Dillon with Mia. She has means and motive.

The Glenwood Glow & Go is a posh salon located on the opposite side of the Colorado River on Grand Avenue. When I arrive, I follow a group of squealing, giggling ladies through the door. They're wearing matching t-shirts except for the woman who wears a white t-shirt with Bride written in gold cursive.

"Right this way, ladies! We have your exclusive suite all ready for you!" the Glow & Go receptionist tells them.

While waiting at the front desk for her to return, I enjoy the plush carpet beneath my feet, the soothing music piped in through the speakers and the slightest hint of a soothing lavender scent. Too bad I'm secretly here on official business. It would be nice to take the day off for a relaxing spa day. Something tells me I'll need one for sure after I determine who killed Dillon. If Dillon was indeed murdered.

"Hi there, I have an appointment with Erica," I tell the receptionist when she returns.

"You can take a seat, and she'll be right with you. Help yourself to a glass of cucumber water while you're waiting."

"Thanks!" What the heck is cucumber water? I fill a paper cup from the large multicolored glass pitcher sitting next to the receptionist's desk, and take a sip. Oh, wow, this is good! How have I not tried this before?

"Excuse me, Holly?" Erica asks when she appears moments later. I'm relieved to discover she doesn't recognize me. I obviously recognize her though. Her dark, wavy hair, green eyes and porcelain skin are hard to forget.

"Yes, I'm Holly."

"Wonderful. Follow me, please. Oh, and you can bring the cucumber water with you," she assures me upon seeing my disappointed look.

"Oh good!" I'm not giving up this drink for anything. Should I ask for the recipe? I assume it's only cucumbers floating in the water, isn't it? Whatever it is, it's amazing.

"What are you looking to do with your hair today, Miss Holly?" she asks.

"It's almost summer, so I thought I'd try something new. Take a few inches off the bottom and maybe add some highlights?" I suggest. "What do you think?"

After pausing to appraise my hair, she gasps. Uh oh. The jig is up. She recognizes me. "Your lavender eyes are beautiful!" she gushes.

"Thank you," I respond. Phew. That was a close one.

"You know what? I recently created this vibrant hair dye especially for highlights. It's plant-based and cruelty free, of course, with a generous dash of magic. The royal purple will be gorgeous with your dark hair, plus it shimmers in the sunlight."

"It sounds great!" I tell her as she drapes a plastic cape over me. "When are you due?" I ask casually.

When she falters I remember the angry welt on Mia's face, and panic a little bit. She's barely showing. I don't think I'd notice if Wendy hadn't told us. Did I speak too soon? Should I have built the conversation up more before jumping in? I hope she doesn't curse me. Or worse. My hair!

"I'm only at 16 weeks," she says, reluctantly.

"Oh, you have a way to go," I respond with a flick of my hand, like I'm not that interested. "You look amazing, by the way."

"Thank you," she says. "Do you have kids?"

"No, not yet. I mean, I'm not even married. I'm a widow, actually."

"Oh, no. But you're so young!"

"Enough about me! You and *your* husband must be thrilled with a little one on the way."

"If you must know, I'm kind of a widow myself."

"What happened? You're too young as well!"

"My boyfriend recently passed away from a heart attack."

"A heart attack? How is that possible?" I hope I'm as convincing to Erica as I sound in my head. If she realizes who I am she'll be mad. There's no telling what she would do.

"It was one of those freak things they can't explain. He was young and healthy - a trainer at the Glenwood Sport Gym - but he collapsed in the middle of a spin class. One minute we were getting ready to have a baby, the next, he was gone," she sniffles.

"I'm so sorry. You must be devastated."

"Yes," she sighs. "But my boyfriend, Dillon, developed a sports drink, which will be available in stores soon. I'm sure his business partner will want me to take over Dillon's part of the company until the baby is older. I bet he'll be a trainer like his dad." She beams.

"You're having a boy?"

"Yes! I just found out!"

"I think you're very brave to keep going like you have. I could barely get out of bed after my husband was killed." I leave out the part where that was the least of it. After that, I got angry. And was asked to leave my job, courtesy of a big severance check.

Not everyone has the same issues I did of course. We all grieve differently, but for someone who is about to become a single parent, she's far more calm than I would be. Aside from her magically cursing Mia at the gym anyway.

"I have to keep going for my baby's sake."

"You said you'll be taking over for your boyfriend in the sports drink business? Does it mean you won't be doing hair anymore?"

"Once the sports drink is available, I imagine I'll have to quit doing hair. Dillon predicted it will be wildly popular.

We have plans to take it national, so I obviously won't have time for hair. My parents want me to move home to Iowa so they can help me with the baby."

"They want you to move home because Dillon died?"

She hesitates. "Yeah, kind of."

"What do you mean?"

"They first urged me to move home while Dillon and I were going through a rough patch. Like any couple, we had our issues, but we worked through them. Besides, I knew once the baby came, we'd be right as rain."

Aside from the part about the baby, she is essentially saying the same things as Mia. What was up with Dillon and these women?

"Relationships are hard." I nod sympathetically. "What do you mean, issues?"

"There was this other girl."

"No!" I exclaim

"Yes, she manipulated him into thinking she understood him so much better than I ever could. But once I told him I was pregnant, he put an end to it. Mercy, will you listen to me; I'm going on and on about myself when you're the client. I'm supposed to be asking about you!"

"It's okay. I'm a bartender, so I know how it goes. But I hope everything works out for you and the baby."

"All done! What do you think?" She twirls the chair around to face the mirror while fluffing my hair to perfection.

"Wow! It's so pretty!" She did an amazing job. Whatever kind of witchcraft she used for the highlights, it's impressive. The dark purple frames my face making my lavender eyes pop. And she's right, the highlights glisten in the light. It's too bad she's a suspect because she's a whiz in the salon. What? It's hard to find someone who really knows hair!

# Chapter 15

Ivan's office is in one of those trendy sharing setups, with several businesses using the wide open space at once, which is surprisingly chaotic. The formerly abandoned warehouse, where they once processed coal from a mine on the west side of town, combines the original rustic design with a modern flair. The atrium is adorned with mid-century modern furniture and strings of lights woven throughout the rafters.

As I worry about how I'll ever find him in the chaos, I spot a large computer screen in front of the concierge desk. It lets visitors enter the name of the person they're looking for to send them a message. Considering I didn't tell Ivan I was coming, nor does he know who I am, I hope that telling him I'm here about Dillon will be enough to coax him out of his office.

"Yes!" I quietly cheer when he says he'll be right down.

"Holly?" he asks when he approaches me a couple minutes later.

"Hi, I'm here about your friend Dillon Watkins."

"You're a lawyer?" he asks, backing away so fast I can almost see protective walls go up. His subdued demeanor, round wire-rimmed glasses, and short stature make him almost the opposite of Dillon. They must make an interesting looking pair.

"No, are you expecting one?"

"I've been waiting for them to show up ever since he died."

"Oh, you mean one of Erica's lawyers."

"Who's Erica?" he asks.

How can he not know who Erica is if he and Dillon were close friends? Besides, Erica talked like it was a done deal. What's going on here?

"She's the woman who's pregnant with Dillon's baby."

"Oh, great. Let me guess. Now she thinks she owns part of my business."

I brush my newly highlighted hair away from my face. This is rather embarrassing. Was Erica conning me? "Kind of. She told me that she's planning to help you run the company for now, and when the baby grows up, *he'll* run it."

"Lady, are you for real?"

"Yes?" I'm not sure how to answer a question like that.

"So you *are* a lawyer?"

"No…" Oh dear, how do I explain this? "I'm actually a Paranormal Private Investigator, not a lawyer but I think if Dillon helped develop the sports drink and owns half the company, it's only fair his child benefit."

"Developed? Developed?" Ivan laughs cruelly. "Dillon's contribution, aside from his fan base, was to suggest we make a bacon-flavored sports drink, which obviously didn't happen."

"When he talked about it, he made it sound like he was a co-inventor or something." Did he tell Erica the same thing? Is that why she thinks she could share the business?

"I'm sure you're not the only person he told that to. Wait, you're another one of his groupies. Or girlfriends. Or whatever. I lost track after a while."

"No, no, no! Absolutely not!" I wave my hands about. "I barely knew the guy. But do you mind if I ask, what's so special about this drink? There's a lot of them on the market. How is yours different?"

"Obviously, I can't go into detail, trade secrets and all that. But basically, I developed a compound which cuts out half the sugar and sodium without adding artificial sweeteners."

"Yet it's still tasty?" I'm skeptical.

"Of course! And refreshing. Unlike Dillon's bacon-flavored plan. You see, your traditional sports drinks provide the most advantage for hardcore athletes. The sugar and sodium in those formulas are geared toward a triathlete, for instance. Not so much the average person who maybe spends a little time on the treadmill or mowing the lawn, but wants something other than water or pop to drink. It's for your everyday kind of active person. The guy or girl who takes a spin class and wants a refreshing beverage with more taste than plain water, but doesn't want all the sugar and salt."

"I don't know much about sports drinks." I nod. "But it sounds like a pretty big deal."

"It's a huge deal," he assures me.

"And Dillon contributed little to developing this?"

"Right. I'm not saying I didn't need him. Quite the contrary, I needed him to advertise and promote the drink. But the way he ran around town, bragging about how he developed it, really bugged me."

"What happens now that he's gone? Who will you get to promote it?" I ask.

"Good question. It's a big problem. When I told him to stop telling people he developed the formula, he threatened to withdraw his support."

"It made you mad."

"I was furious. But just because he didn't help me develop the drink didn't mean I didn't need his reach and popularity to help market it. It's one thing to sell it in the shops in Glenwood Springs, but it's a different challenge altogether to go national, like we're hoping to do. So far, no one will take a chance on us. The bigger grocery store chains tell me they want to wait and see how it goes here first. If it does gangbusters in town, like I think it will, we're looking at national distribution as early as next year."

"How long did you know Dillon?" I ask.

"Since we were kids."

"Was he always an athlete?"

"Are you kidding me? He was a chubby, nerdy kid who everyone picked on. One day in the cafeteria, after some kids knocked his lunch tray out of his hands, I invited him to sit with me in a storage area no one else knew about and share my lunch."

"They picked on you too."

"Kids are mean." He nods.

Don't I know it!

"I'm still not sure why you're here, but I have to excuse myself. I'm already late for a meeting," he tells me.

"Yes, of course. I'm so sorry. Thank you for your time!" I tell him when he hurries off to his meeting.

As I head for the door, planning my next move, my phone dings with a text. It's Gabe. Maybe he has the ashes!

**My friend at the post office told me the package is already on its way to Wyoming, but he gave me the tracking number. If anyone asks, we didn't get it from him! But this way, you can monitor it, and when it arrives in Wyoming, contact Dillon's parents. I'm sorry, but it's the best I can do.**

**No problem! Thanks for checking.**

As I leave Ivan's office, the air hints of rain and I gaze up at the clouds, noting the impending storm. The weatherman warned it would be a big one. Any lightning storm in Glenwood brings real fear of forest fires.

One of the first trails I hiked after moving here, was the Storm King Mountain Memorial Trail, where 14 firefighters once perished battling a deadly blaze. One ill-timed lightening bolt can have deadly consequences in a place surrounded by evergreen trees.

Often, after a heavy storm, the authorities close Glenwood Canyon, the only direct route east of Glenwood. When it closes, we have to either wait it out, or take a more circuitous route, which can add hours to the commute. If the truck carrying the ashes left the canyon already, they should be on their way to Wyoming right now.

The sooner they arrive, the sooner I can contact Dillon's parents. My stomach twists into nervous knots, thinking about what I'll say to them. They lost their son, and now

I want his ashes because there's a possibility he was mur-dered. That should be a fun conversation. For now, I must have a different fun conversation. Confronting Dillon.

# Chapter 16

The moment I climb out of the VW in the gym parking lot, big raindrops splash on my head. I make a run for it, but before I get to the door, the heavens open with a torrential downpour. For once, the weather matches my mood.

"Hey, you did something different with your hair!" Dillon says the moment I march through the front door, ready to confront him about everything I've learned.

"You would not be talking like that if you knew the mood I was in," I growl. "And you're pretty much why my hair, along with the rest of me, is soaked."

"Excuse me, miss, can I help you?" a confused desk clerk asks.

"Yes, in a moment," I tell him dripping water in the entryway. "Actually, could I please have a towel? Or several?"

"Sure?" he tells me, still looking perplexed.

"I was talking about the purple in your hair, not the wet part," Dillon's ghost says.

"If you must know, Erica did my hair."

"You saw Erica? What did she say?" he asks excitedly. "I feel so cooped up in this gym. I want news from the outside world."

"She told me you're the baby's father, but since you're gone, she'll have to help Ivan run the sports drink company until the baby is old enough to take over."

Dillon's spirit stares at me open-mouthed for so long, I'm convinced he's stuck like that. But when he doubles over guffawing, I'm furious. This is no laughing matter.

"You think this is funny?" I chastise him.

"No, miss, I don't," the desk clerk tells me when he returns with several towels and a mop for the wet mess I'm making on the floor.

"Sorry. I wasn't talking to you," I explain. "But thanks for the towels!" Luckily, the phone rings before he can ask me *who* I'm talking to. "Let's step over to the side where we're out of the way," I tell Dillon. I hope the phone call takes a while because I don't have a plausible story for the clerk if he comes back. My wet shoes make squishing noises when we move, and I cringe at the mess I'm making.

"It's so far from the truth I don't know where to start," Dillon insists.

"Try from the beginning!" I throw up my arms in frustration but remind myself to take deep calming breaths when several people nearby pause their conversation to look at us. Or me, I should say, since they can't see Dillon.

"Okay, okay, I apologize for laughing. Erica clearly has issues and I shouldn't make fun of her."

"*I* still want to know how *you* know it isn't true," I whisper loudly, as if it will prevent people from gawking at me.

"I made her take a paternity test!" he exclaims.

"How do you take a paternity test before the baby is born?" He's bluffing, right?

"It's a simple blood test. Something to do with the baby's cells being in the mother's blood or some sort of scientific thingy."

I'm still skeptical. He has to be making this up.

"You can look it up on the internet!" he continues.

"*If* I believe you, and that's a big *if*, *who* is the father?"

"No clue. I just know it isn't me."

"This might sound dumb, but Erica knows, too, right?"

"Yes! We got the results in the doctor's office. When she found out I wasn't the father, she tore up the test results in front of me and threw them on the ground."

"Why does she still insist you're the father?" I ask. None of this makes sense.

"Maybe because I'm dead? Who's going to tell, right?"

"Good point. Do you think she was mad enough to poison you?"

"I hadn't stopped to think of that. Maybe? But now that you mention it, maybe?"

"She's also a witch," I remind him, "she could have created a poison, like she did the purple highlights in my hair."

"They look very nice." He nods in agreement.

"Truthfully, I'll be disappointed if she killed you. I like what she did for my hair."

"Who else did you talk to? You have such a fun job, by the way."

"Yes, it's a real gas. I met Ivan."

"What did he say?"

"What do you think he said?"

"Ohhh, you're turning the tables on me. That's clever."

"Mmm hmm." I stare at him, waiting for him to speak.

"Did he tell you we've been friends since we were kids?"

"He did." I pause again while he shifts uncomfortably. Who could have imagined? Even ghosts get nervous.

"He isn't too happy with me, is he?"

"Nope."

"All right, I admit it; I may have exaggerated a little when I said I helped him develop the sports drink formula. But I still think a bacon-flavored drink is a fabulous idea. He's going to release the drink like we planned though, isn't he? He can't drop it because I'm dead. Please tell me he isn't quitting."

"He's still selling the drink, but without your face, of course."

"Hey, don't you think he should still use me? My picture, I mean?"

"Ehhh, I don't think that's the best idea."

"But why? My legend would live on! How cool is that?"

"He'd be marketing a drink with the face of a young athlete who dropped dead from a heart attack," I point out.

"Technically, it was murder," he reminds me.

"Was Ivan mad enough to kill you?" I ask, ignoring his need to be a star, even in the afterlife. "He's familiar with chemistry, obviously. I assume he could poison you."

"He was really mad at me too," he acknowledges. "My bailing on the marketing end would have cost him a lot of sales."

"Is it true you were a chubby kid everyone picked on?"

"Oh, yeah. That."

"But you started working out, got braces, learned how to dress like the cool kids, so you got popular and left Ivan behind."

"Hey, I tried to bring him along!"

"But he didn't care for your new friends."

"Not really. Eventually, we drifted apart. Except for the new drink."

"I met Theo too."

"You've been busy!"

"I have been busy, but I'm spinning my wheels at this point. You've made quite a few enemies for such a young guy. When were you going to tell me you were firing him?"

"I wasn't firing Theo! Where did you hear that?"

"He told me!"

"Where did *he* hear it?"

"I don't know."

"Didn't you ask him?"

"He may have been a little drunk," I admit.

"There's your answer. He didn't know what he was saying."

"But he didn't look happy with you at the celebration of life either."

"I didn't notice," he says.

"I'm sure you didn't. He also said he thinks Ivan killed you."

"Now I know you're pulling my leg!" he laughs. "You think if Theo was convinced I was firing him, it would give him motive to kill me?"

"Yes."

"Hmmm, people are mad at me, aren't they?"

"Would Theo know how to poison you?"

"Not a clue. Who else is mad at me? This is like a big puzzle," he says a little too enthusiastically.

I swear if he's just doing this for the attention I will... I will... okay, I don't know what I'll do, but I'll be furious.

"Mia came by the bookstore."

"Oh, yeah, her."

"Yes, her," I glare at him for a moment, "Wendy gave her a potion for the nasty rash Erica cursed her with."

"Oh yeah, it looked bad. I'm glad Wendy had something for it. Erica can be touchy."

"Gee, I wonder why. Also, Mia seems to think you were moving to Texas with her."

He rubs the back of his neck, looking sheepish, but says nothing.

"If I had an accurate list of all the women you were stringing along, I bet it would take me a year to interview everyone who had motive to kill you. You know, Mia and Erica had eerily similar things to say - each thought you had dumped the other one and were committed to them."

"I have a hard time breaking up with women." He shrugs.

"So you had no plans to move to Texas with Mia and supposedly operate the sports drink business there?"

"No?"

"And you had no plans to move to Iowa with Erica and the baby and operate the business from there."

"No?"

"Why do your answers sound like questions?"

"Uhhh, I don't know?"

What is it with these women falling for this nonsense? "Did you specifically tell these women you were moving with them and were committed to them or not?"

"Absolutely not!"

"Why do they both insist you were? I find it suspicious two women could have invented the same scenario."

"It's not like I told them I was moving with them; but I may have hinted around about something like it. I wanted them to quit asking me where the relationship was going."

"Hinted how?" I'm beginning to see why the list of suspects is so long.

"I might have said something like, 'if I'm moving to Texas, I'll need a good pair of cowboy boots.' That sort of thing."

"Instead of simply telling these poor women 'no, it's never going to happen,' you let them believe it was a possibility."

"Well, when you put it like that."

"Why did you do that?" I ask, my voice raising in frustration.

"If I said no, they'd be mad at me. I hate it when people are mad at me. Especially women."

"But it was the truth."

"But they'd be mad at me. Did you miss that part?"

"But by not being honest with them, you may have driven them to murder!" I'm yelling at this point.

"Well if I'd known that, I would have said no."

# Chapter 17

With the VW's windshield wipers working overtime I squint through the pounding rain and hail. Driving home in this vicious storm wasn't the best idea. But I know Clara will be a nervous wreck waiting for me to come home. Thankfully, everyone else braving the monsoon is creeping along as carefully as I am.

I didn't realize my house was haunted until after I bought it. I met up with the listing agent for the keys and saw Clara for the first time, watching me from the picture window. Admittedly, I said some rude things at the time that I now regret. I was still reeling over my abrupt dismissal from my job, the unexpected move to Colorado, and grieving profoundly over Ben's death, although I refused to admit it. Even to myself.

Of course, the sellers couldn't see her like I can, but from what she's told me about the tricks she liked to play on them, they undoubtedly sensed there was a ghost in the house. It's rumored she convinced them there were several!

I still say they should disclose any other-worldly presence before they sell! But here I am, surprised to realize how oddly comforting it is to have someone at home worrying about me.

When I finally pull into the garage, exhausted but in one piece, I breathe a sigh of relief. Which quickly turns to a scream when Clara appears unannounced in the backseat of the bus.

"Where have you been?" she shrieks with the same tone as Mrs. Weasley when the boys arrive home in the flying car after rescuing Harry on his birthday. Minus the British accent of course. "I was worried sick!"

"I had to drive extra slowly in the storm," I explain.

"You should have called!"

"How? It's not like you have a cell phone."

"Maybe you should get me one."

"No. I'm not getting a ghost a cell phone." I can't believe we're having this conversation. "But how about this? I brought you a book from Wendy's store," I tell her, waving an Agatha Christie novel in front of her. "You mentioned you hadn't read this one."

"Wonderful!" she shouts!

Nothing like a good book to take your mind off your current worries, right?

"Don't forget to bring it inside," she adds.

"I won't."

She's been pestering me to bring home more books for her to read. Even though she and Mystery watch a lot of TV, she tells me she misses going to the library. Luckily for her, and for me, she can turn her own pages.

"You'll need your umbrella to get to the house," she warns.

"Thanks," I tell her, rolling my eyes. "I hadn't noticed."

"I mean for the book, silly. We don't want it to get wet, do we?"

Of course not.

Clara disappears again, I assume back into the house, while I check the bus for any hail damage. Oh, how the tide has turned. I've gone from thinking of this bus as a nuisance to being worried that it was marred by hail.Once I'm satisfied everything looks all right, I fight my way into the house. The wind is so bad it nearly rips the umbrella from my hands.

I finally make it inside, dripping wet once again. I make a beeline for the stove, where I turn the dial for the burner with a satisfying whoosh, then put the kettle on for tea to warm myself up. I never had a gas stove and while I admit it scared me at first, I now love it. It reminds me of the stove my grandparents had. Next, I pull a fluffy towel from the dryer to dry some of the excess water off me, so I don't track it onto the original wood flooring.

"Whatcha watching?" I ask Clara and Mystery, who are glued to the TV as usual.

"The news. The Canyon is closed because of a rock slide," Clara informs me.

"I was afraid of that," I tell her.

"Check it out. A mail truck overturned on the highway." Mystery points a fluffy paw at the screen.

"A what?" I hurry over to see what she's talking about. My stomach flip-flops with anxiety when I see the large mail truck tipped over on its side just as the teakettle whistles ominously.

"Be careful, dear. You're dripping water on the floor," Clara points out.

"Is the driver okay?"

"They said they took him to the hospital with minor injuries."

"That's good. Considering it was tipped over like that. It must have been scary for him." That wasn't the truck with the ashes, was it? Nah. What are the odds of that? Although I have a sinking feeling that with my luck it would be. I briefly picture the ashes falling out of the back end, bouncing down the hill, then tumbling with a loud splash into the rushing Colorado River below, floating away, and disappearing forever.

"Your water is ready," Clara reminds me as the kettle still whistles impatiently.

Huh? Oh. Yeah. The tea.

Shortly after the storm lets up, Wendy texts me

**Have you heard anything from Mia?**

**No. But I don't have her phone number. I take it you haven't heard anything?**

**Nope. But I have her address.**

**I think we should pay our friend Mia a visit. I have some questions for her.**

**Pick me up at the bookstore!**

Not only is Mia still a suspect, but I think she may be able to help me with some questions I have about poisonous substances in general. And I'm sure Wendy wants to see how her cure is progressing.

So far, Mia and Ivan are the most likely suspects on my list. I'm convinced they would know how to poison someone, and make it look like a heart attack. They also have a strong motive for wanting Dillon dead. For different reasons, of course, but they're both pretty angry.

When we arrive at Mia's studio apartment, I assume she's home because her door is cracked open. Does she always leave it like that? That's unsafe!

"Hello?" I call out softly while rapping my knuckles on the door jam.

"Mia? Are you in there? It's Wendy and Holly from the bookstore!" Wendy leans in to shout.

When her door creaks open a little more, I jump back. I don't want to startle her. What if she thinks we're burglars?

"Mia! We're wondering how your face is doing," Wendy says.

"She's not here," her next-door neighbor tells us after peeking her head out of the door.

"But her door was open."

"I haven't seen her for a couple of days."

I push the door open a little more, screaming at the horrific sight in front of me.

"What is it?" the neighbor asks, running to join us.

"Her apartment has been ransacked! We have to call the Sheriff! She might be injured. Or dead!"

"Oh, it always looks like this," the neighbor assures us. "I'm Blair, by the way."

"But you said you haven't seen her for awhile, so why was her door open? I assume she doesn't leave it like that when she's gone," I point out.

"Yeah, her place is a disaster most of the time, but she definitely doesn't leave the door open when she's gone," the neighbor admits. "Do you think something happened to her? She told me last week she thought someone was following her. It made her nervous, so I know she wouldn't just leave the door open if she wasn't home."

"We're calling the Sheriff!" Wendy and I exclaim in unison.

# Chapter 18

"**S**heriff Mack!" I exclaim when he arrives at Mia's studio apartment. I self-consciously fuss with my hair until I catch Wendy staring at me, with one eyebrow raised in amusement. Why am I worried about my hair at a time like this? "I'm so glad you came," I tell him.

"This better be good. I was in the middle of something important," he grunts.

"Mia Nunez is missing!" I blurt out.

"Yes, you said that over the phone. But how do you know she's missing?" he asks, peering into her apartment. "Jeepers, it's been ransacked. You didn't go in there, did you? Step back and wait for me over there while I call in the investigative team," he insists, pushing us to the side. "Do you know what the burglars were looking for?"

When I open my mouth to speak, he holds up a finger. "Darius, Mack here. I need a forensics team at...hang on a sec...what is it?" he asks when he sees us waving at him to stop.

"Her apartment always looks like it's been ransacked," Blair insists, while Wendy and I nod vigorously.

"Who are you?"

"I'm her neighbor, Blair Becker."

"Darius," he returns to his call. "Never mind. I'll call you back."

"You're telling me," he says, pushing the door open wide to further reveal the disaster in Mia's apartment, "this isn't the work of criminals, but she normally lives like this."

"Uh huh." Blair nods.

"So you don't know for certain she's missing?"

"Wellll," Wendy wriggles her hand.

"I can see it's a studio apartment, but did you check the bathroom?"

"No, I didn't think of it," I gulp. Why didn't I think to check the bathroom after Blair said she hadn't seen her? What if she's lying there unconscious and we've been standing out here chatting? I think I'm going to be sick. How could I be so stupid?

"Stay here! All of you. I mean it!" he scolds.

After winding his way through the cluttered obstacle course, he peers into the bathroom. My heart thuds in my chest so hard I'm surprised the others don't hear it. I let out a grateful sigh of relief when he shakes his head indicating she isn't there either.

"I was so scared for a second there," Wendy says while Blair and I nod in agreement.

"Let's try this again," he says after making his way back to us. "How certain are you she's actually missing and didn't just go to Grand Junction or Denver for the weekend?"

Wendy wriggles her hand again.

He sighs loudly, folding his arms across his chest while taking his determined, 'this better be good' stance I've become all too familiar with. "Start talking," he demands.

"As you know, I'm looking into a," I glance at Blair, hesitant about saying too much in front of a stranger, "suspicious death recently. You also know I had a conversation with Mia--"

"Mia was murdered?" Blair exclaims.

"Now I didn't say that," I tell her. "Besides, if I knew she'd been murdered, why would I be here looking for her?"

"You mean she's a suspect in someone else's murder?" she gasps.

"Calm down; I didn't say that either."

"You said suspicious death. If that's not murder, I don't know what is!" she protests. "Should I be concerned? Am I living next to a murderer and didn't know it? Why don't the cops notify us about these things?" she shouts, pointing at Sheriff Mack. Her voice gets louder and higher pitched by the syllable. "The least you could do is send out a warning! I stream CSI all the time. I know how these things go. It's always the last person you suspect."

"Miss, will you excuse us, please? I promise, if we determine you're in danger, you'll be the first one we contact," he assures her in his most measured manner.

"Okay, if you're sure," she responds, drifting toward her apartment.

"I'm sure." He nods.

"I'm holding you to it!" she shouts.

After we hear her apartment door click, Sheriff Mack turns to me. "Talk."

"I talked to Dillon--"

"--you mean Dillon's ghost," he interrupts, then shakes his head like he can't believe he said that.

"Yes, I talked to Dillon's ghost again, and after he contradicted several of the stories other people have told me, I decided to reach out to Mia to ask her about what Dillon said."

"And *I* wanted to find out how her rash was doing!" Wendy adds.

"Right." I look at her, nodding. "I also wanted to ask her about how someone would poison a person but make it look like a heart attack."

"Because she's a chemistry major," the Sheriff says.

"Yes, exactly. Wendy had her address, so we thought it would be best to talk to her in person. But she wasn't here, and her door was partially opened."

"But Ms." he checks his notes, "Becker claims it always looks like that," he reminds us.

"Inside, yes, but she also insisted she hadn't seen her in days and while her apartment is always a mess, she'd never leave the door open when she's gone."

"Don't forget the part where she was sure someone was following her," Wendy adds.

"Excuse me?" Sheriff Mack asks, suddenly looking very alert.

"Yes, I was getting to that. The neighbor said Mia was concerned someone was following her. Add to the fact she hasn't seen her in a while and Wendy hasn't heard from her either, along with the open door we decided to contact you."

Sheriff Mack groans, while pinching the bridge of his nose. "You could have led with the stalker part."

"But I wanted to make sure you got the entire story," I tell him. Now I'm embarrassed. He's right. I probably should have started with the scariest part first.

When Wendy notices my embarrassment, she cuts in. "We thought we should *end* with the most dramatic part."

"Uh-huh. Do either of you know where Mia normally hangs out? Aside from her apartment or the gym, I suppose."

"The university, maybe?" Wendy suggests.

"We could ask the neighbor," I add. "I'll do it," I volunteer when I see him cringe at the thought of talking to Blair again.

I barely get the first knock in when she throws the door open. "What is it? I'm in danger, aren't I? I knew it. You aren't going to tell me to just stay inside and lock the door, are you? Because it never seems to work well on tv. Does the Sheriff's Department have a safe house where they send people like me?"

"Uhhh, no, do you happen to know where Mia normally hangs out? Aside from her apartment."

"Oh! You know what? She spends a lot of time at the university lab. She tells me sometimes she starts working in the morning and then doesn't realize it's already night and she hasn't eaten all day! Maybe that's why she hasn't been around. She might be in the lab working!" she exclaims.

Now *I'm* thinking the neighbor should have started with that.

"Thank you! You've been a big help!" I tell her.

"You'll let me know how this turns out, won't you?" she calls after us.

I hold my thumb in the air while we run toward Sheriff Mack. Assuming we find Mia in one piece, I'll make sure she checks in with her.

"Let's start with the university!" I tell him.

"Lets? Like all of us?" he asks.

"You're the one who refused to treat this like a crime when I first told you Dillon said he was murdered," I remind him.

"Fine. You can ride with me. Nice hair, by the way."

I don't dare look at Wendy. I don't want to see the smug look I know will be there. "He wouldn't have come in person for just anybody," Wendy whispers in my ear on the way to the Sheriff's squad car.

"Mind your own business!" I hiss back.

# Chapter 19

After we arrive at the university, I realize I haven't the foggiest idea of where to look for Mia. The chemistry department? But where is it?

"Where do we go now?" I ask my friends. Sheriff Mack is a friend, right? Kind of?

"You said she's a chemistry major? She might be in the labs," he says.

"I don't know where those are."

"They're on the other side of campus," he explains, pointing in the opposite direction.

When I stare at him dumbfounded, his jaw clenches. "You thought a dumb cop wouldn't know his way around a college campus?"

"That's not what I was thinking," I stammer while Wendy is conveniently fascinated by a sidewalk crack. Some help she is.

"I have dual degrees in Criminal Justice and Forensic Science. With straight A's, I might add. Although it was some time ago," he says, appearing amused at the memories.

"I don't know what to say," I tell him. I have a hard time picturing the Sheriff as a college student. Certainly not because I thought he was uneducated, but the idea of him riding a bike across campus or playing frisbee with friends in the quad strikes me as humorous. I can't quite picture Surly Steve in that way.

"We're here to find Mia," Wendy gently reminds us.

"Follow me," Sheriff Mack says.

In the science building, we follow arrows pointing to the chemistry lab, which is in the basement. It's eerily quiet down here. The only sounds come from our foot steps trodding along the corridor. We pass a ghost with a nasty head wound who waves at me. I wave back, but hurry on my way. I'm curious about how he got the injury - considering it must have killed him - but we have to focus on finding Mia right now.

"This is like looking for a needle in a haystack," Wendy says, as we stare at the many doors lining the hallway, all individually numbered.

"Should we each pick a door?" I ask. I turn back to ask the ghost if he's seen Mia, but he disappeared already.

"Wait?" Sheriff Mack says, raising his hand to silence us.

"I don't--"

"Shhh!" he warns. "Someone is calling for help!"

"I hear pounding!" Wendy says. "From that way!" She points down the hall.

We run toward the sound until we reach the door where it's loudest. The Sheriff insists we wait in the hallway as he draws his gun, carefully pushing open the unlocked door. Naturally, we ignore him, piling into the room after him.

"Let me out of here! Help! Let me out!"

"That sounds like Mia!" Wendy says.

With a few of purposeful strides, Sheriff Mack crosses the lab. His gun still poised, he pauses in front of a door labeled Supplies. "It's locked!" he says after attempting to turn the knob. But when he twists the lock in the middle of the doorknob, and opens the door, Mia tumbles out.

"Oh, thank goodness! I was really freaking out!" she exclaims.

"What were you doing in there?" I ask. "Did you lock yourself in?"

She stares at me like I'm a bonehead. "Of course not! Someone locked me in!"

"On purpose?" Wendy asks.

"Yes!" Mia practically shouts. "The moment I heard the door lock I immediately pounded on it and shouted. There's no way they didn't hear me."

"How long were you in there?" Sheriff Mack asks.

"Several hours at least. I left my phone on the table so I'm not sure of the time. If you'll excuse me, I need to use the bathroom!" she declares, rushing from the room.

"Why would the door only lock from the outside?" Wendy asks, kneeling down to examine the doorknob.

"Someone may have used it as a replacement. Or installed it incorrectly to begin with. Hard to say." Sheriff Mack shrugs.

After several minutes, Mia returns. "What are you all doing here by the way?"

"We were looking for you," I tell her.

"For me? Why?"

"We were worried you'd gone missing," Wendy adds.

"How did you know I was missing? I barely know you."

"We went to your apartment to check on your rash," Wendy tells her. "Your face looks good, by the way. I can barely tell anything happened."

"Oh!" Mia says, placing a hand to her cheek. "I was so engrossed in my work I almost forgot about it. I can barely feel it now. What a relief. I appreciate your checking up on me, but what made you come all the way down here?"

"I also had some follow-up questions," I tell her.

"Questions? About wh-- oh no, it's gone!" she cries.

"What's gone?" Wendy asks.

"The bottle!" she exclaims, frantically searching the workbench which is covered in handwritten notes.

"What bottle?" the Sheriff asks.

"Dillon's bottle!" she screeches on the verge of panicking.

"You had Dillon's bottle?" I ask. Mia's the killer? Of course, in my mind, she was the most obvious suspect, given her chemistry background, and the fact Dillon lied to her. But to have her confirm it like this is a little surprising.

She pauses when she realizes we're all staring at her dumbstruck. A sheepish look crosses her face. "I took it after he died," she admits.

"Because you poisoned it!" I insist.

"I what?"

"You poisoned Dillon's drink on purpose because you were mad he wasn't moving to Texas with you, and you were worried he was the father of Erica's baby."

"Are you drunk?" she asks, crooking her head at me, thoroughly confused.

I sigh when I realize It's time to come clean. "I know we only met at the Looking Glass the other day, but my name is Holly Daniel. I'm a paranormal private investigator and a spirit communicator."

She pauses for a moment before realizing what that means. "You see dead people?"

"Yes."

"Butterscotch gumdrops, you've seen Dillon's spirit!" she exclaims with surprise.  Have you talked to him? What did he say? Does he miss me? Can you take me to him? Where is he?" Questions tumble from her mouth like a rushing waterfall.

But when I open *my* mouth to answer, she continues.

"What do you mean, he wasn't moving to Texas with me?"

I try again to answer. "And what do you mean he's the father of Erica's baby? He told me he wasn't!"

Interesting those are the first things she's concerned about, and *not* Dillon being poisoned.

I open my mouth again, and this time when she doesn't interrupt, I continue. "Yes, I've talked to Dillon's ghost. He's at the gym where he died."

"Can you tell him to come here? I need to talk to him!"

"His spirit can't leave the gym."

"So he'll be stuck there forever?"

Where do I even start? "Did you hear the part where I said he was poisoned?"

"Wait. Poisoned? When?"

"His drink was spiked - at least, that's what he thinks - in his bottle."

"But they said he died from a heart attack!"

"It's kind of why I was looking for you. I wondered what type of poison would give someone a heart attack?"

Mia's stunned expression makes me think she didn't poison Dillon after all.

"I didn't find any poison in the bottle. But I wasn't finished with my tests. Wait!" She exclaims. "It might be... never mind," she says after checking under the microscope. "It's gone."

"What's gone?"

"The sample I was examining."

"You're saying you didn't poison Dillon's drink?" I press. "You didn't kill Dillon?"

"Why would I? He was finally ready to commit to me. We were talking about moving to Texas together..." she trails off. "You're legit talking to his ghost?"

Now I feel bad. I blurted those things out, assuming she was the killer, and took the bottle to keep anyone from finding out. It would have been better for her to think Dillon loved her. She could have moved on with her life in ignorant bliss. Now she knows what a scoundrel he truly was.

"Yes, I'm afraid so," I tell her.

"Has he asked about me? Does he miss me?"

"We've talked about you."

"What did he say?"

"I…" I look to the Sheriff and Wendy for help. Can't they say something to get me off the hook?

"I have some questions, Miss Nunez." Sheriff Mack steps forward.

"Okay."

I'm relieved when he pulls out his notebook. "Is it true you believe someone was stalking you?"

"Yes. I *thought* someone was following me. Now that I've been locked in the supply closet and Dillon's bottle was stolen, I *know* I was being followed."

# Chapter 20

"Can you describe the person following you? Man? Woman?"

"Maybe it's a man? I've only seen him lurking from a distance. I don't know. Maybe it's a woman. I can't tell."

"In a car?"

"No, I haven't seen a car. He wears a green hoodie and sunglasses."

"Why haven't you reported this to the Sheriff's Department?"

"I wasn't certain he was following me until now. I thought it might have been my imagination. I was worried you'd think I was being paranoid."

"How long has this been going on?"

Mia pauses for a moment to think. "It started after Dillon died."

"So, after you stole the water bottle," I point out.

"If you want to be exact, yes." Mia nods.

"Do you know if this person in the green hoodie is the one who locked you in the supply closet?" the Sheriff continues.

"I didn't see anyone. But like I said before. I know they heard me."

When my phone rings, I move to silence it. No way I'm missing any of this conversation. But when I realize it's Gabe, I answer it. He always texts instead of calling so it must be important. He may need me to work tonight.

"Hey boss!" I answer.

"You're never going to believe this."

"Considering I see ghosts and--" I cut myself off before I accidentally slip and say my boss is a shifter. It's still only a rumor. Yet people in town have happily been telling wild stories about how they're sure they saw him in wolf form, running through the forest late at night.

No one knows for certain except Gabe. I don't care either way. I've never knowingly met a shifter, so I know little about them. Yes, you'd think a ghost whisperer would know all about these things, but I really don't.

"And?" he asks.

"And witches!" I exclaim. Phew. Nice save. "So there isn't much I don't believe."

"Good point. But this isn't paranormal news. It's mail truck news."

"The ashes have arrived in Wyoming already?"

"Nope! They're back in Glenwood Springs."

"So, they *were* on the truck that overturned in Glenwood Canyon!"

"You knew about that?"

"It was on the news. Have you heard anything more about the driver? They said he went to the hospital."

"According to my friend at the post office, he's home resting. He needed a handful of stitches on his forehead, but otherwise, he's fine. The doctor recommended he take a couple days off."

"That's good to know. I need those ashes!"

"My friend tells me they expect Glenwood Canyon will be closed for another day while they clear the rock slide. But once it opens, they're back on a truck and headed to Wyoming."

"Could he delay them?" I'm trying to picture how I can tell Dillon's parents to let me have the ashes so I can take them for testing. There's no way that's an easy conversation.

"He said if you want the cremains, you'll have to get a court order which could take a while, of course, or the Sheriff's Department could request them."

I stare at Sheriff Mack, who watches me back. I stick my tongue out at Wendy when I catch her observing both of us with an amused look. That girl needs to get a life.

"I'll work on it," I tell him.

"Okay, I have to go now. I sense a fight brewing between busboys, and I better stop it before it gets any worse."

"Thanks for letting me know. I appreciate it!"

"Any time, H."

H? Huh. That's new. I'm not telling Wendy, Gabe now has a nickname for me. I can only imagine what she'll say about it. Especially after she tells Juliet.

"Why don't I give you ladies a ride back to Mia's apartment? That way I can check for any problems and look for clues," Sheriff Mack says.

"I have a favor to ask," I tell him.

"Uh oh." He frowns.

"It's not a big one!" I insist.

"It isn't?"

"Not super big?"

"What is it?" he sighs, once again giving me the arms across the chest, and feet planted position reminding me to tread carefully.

"You obviously know about the rock slide in Glenwood Canyon."

"I do."

"And you know about the mail truck that overturned."

"Yes. Go on."

Wendy shifts uncomfortably as she waits for me to drop the bomb.

I lower my voice, beckoning the Sheriff to come closer because I don't want Mia to overhear the next part. He scoffs dismissively, already expecting he won't like what I have to say.

"Dillon Watkins' ashes were on the overturned mail truck headed to his parents house in Wyoming." I pause, gazing up at him, hoping he'll make the suggestion himself, so I don't have to ask. But when he surveys me silently, I press on. "I need the ashes. Or should I say *we* need the ashes?" Perhaps if he feels like he's a part of this, he'll be more likely to go along with it.

"I know what you're getting at. The packages are back at the Glenwood Post Office."

"They are."

"You were just talking to Gabe about it." He says Gabe like it leaves an unpleasant taste in his mouth.

"Yes. His friend at the post office said they aren't leaving until Glenwood Canyon re-opens. But if we want them tested, your department will have to take custody of them."

"I already told you that's an expensive test."

"Yes, but someone is clearly after Mia in addition to Dillon's bottle. Don't you think it warrants a careful look at his remains?"

"Let me see what I can do. You better be right about this."

When I try to listen in on the Sheriff's phone call from the hallway, Mia rounds on me. "I want to talk to Dillon! He and I have things to discuss."

Rats. Somehow, I was hoping she had already forgotten about that. I know, ridiculous, but hope springs eternal. Thankfully, before I have to say anything further, the Sheriff approaches us. That was quick. The answer must be no.

"I sent a deputy to the post office to collect the ashes. He'll send them to our forensic toxicology lab for testing. If you've sent me on a wild goose chase, I won't be happy. I don't need the county commissioners on my back for wasting money on a test because a paranormal private investigator has a hunch."

"After what we witnessed here, Sheriff, I guarantee they'll find poison," I tell him.

# Chapter 21

"Hey, Clara! I'm going for a run!" I call out while lacing up my running shoes.

"You mean you're going to the bakery for a donut," Mystery scoffs, sauntering through the living room, her tail held high. Even as a ghost cat, she's so haughty.

"I am not!" I exclaim.

"Are so!" Mystery fires back.

"Say hello to Juliet!" Clara shouts on my way out the door.

Why must spirit roommates be so annoying?

I pause on the spacious patio, surveying the quiet neighborhood surrounding my home. I pause, filling my lungs with the fresh mountain air of a beautiful spring morning. The faint sulfur scent from the hot springs is barely noticeable. When I first moved here, the unusual aroma stood out wherever I went.

Everyone assured me I wouldn't detect it after a while, and they were right. Now it just smells like home. After last night's soft rain, the air is especially clean, the rush of the Colorado River beckons in the background. None of it ever gets old.

I run slowly this morning, admiring the beauty of the Colorado mountains. When I finally reach the Grand Avenue Bridge, stretching over the Colorado River, connecting pedestrians to downtown Glenwood Springs, I laugh at myself. Of course, I'm going to Juliet's bakery. But I'm not getting a donut. I'll get a turnover instead. Ha! Mystery thinks she's so smart.

"Donut?" Juliet says when I walk in the door, pausing to catch my breath.

"No, I don't want a donut!" I tell her.

"Okayyyy," she responds, waiting to hear what I'll say next.

"I'll have a cherry turnover; thank you very much."

She laughs while placing a luscious turnover with flaky golden layers and plump, ruby-red cherries on a plate. I love my friends here. While they never hesitate to call me out when I've crossed the line, they also tolerate my occasionally darker eccentricities.

"Wendy filled me in on what went down at the lab yesterday," Juliet says. "That's so wild! I'm glad no one was hurt." She hands me the turnover before pushing her turquoise cat glasses back into place. "I take it you've decided Dillon really was poisoned?"

"It certainly looks more likely at this point. Thankfully, Sheriff Mack called in a favor to have the cremains tested at the forensic lab."

"Called in a favor, huh?" she smirks.

"If you and Wendy don't stop insinuating something is going on with the Sheriff and me, I swear I'll..."

"You'll what? Stop eating my pastries?" she says, watching me shovel a bite of turnover in my mouth, groaning when a tart cherry bursts on my tongue.

"Maybe!" I respond. Good thing Clara isn't here to scold me for talking with my mouth full.

"So, what's next? Knowing you, we won't sit around waiting for test results," Juliet says.

"I want to follow up with several things I talked to Dillon's ghost about. Especially his talent agent Theo Barlow."

"Why him?" Juliet asks, while quickly clearing a cluttered table nearby with magic. I wish I could clear the kitchen table at home without moving from my spot on the couch in front of the television. Sometimes I think being a witch would be so much more useful than talking to dead people.

"He went to the hotel bar after the celebration of life and got even drunker than he already was. Then, he announced to me and the entire bar, he killed Dillon."

"Did Sheriff Mack look into it?" she asks aghast.

"Not yet. Like I said, he was drunk, and I'm not sure he knew where he was. When we put him into a cab, he said Ivan killed Dillon."

"So, he was saying random drunken stuff?"

"Maybe. Maybe not."

"What if they *both* killed Dillon?" Juliet asks wide eyed.

"It's possible. Ivan has the chemistry knowledge and they both have motive. Even though Dillon denies wanting to fire Theo."

"Fire him? Who's more believable? Dillon or Theo?"

"Dillon's a player but he was genuinely confused about why I thought he was firing Theo. Then we have Theo who was drunk as a skunk so who knows why he thought Dillon was firing him."

"Theo's office is down the street. Let's take a few pastries and you can say you wanted to check on him. Then we'll figure out a way to question him about Dillon," she offers.

"Juliet, you're brilliant."

She blushes. "What can I say? Everyone loves pastry."

"Hey, Nina!" she calls out to the high school student helping her for the summer. "I'm going out for a bit."

"Have fun!" Nina says.

While Juliet folds her signature bright yellow takeout box, with a picture of a sparkling sun on top. I gawk at the display case, wondering which ones she'll pick.

"You already had one!" she reminds me.

"Hi, can I help you?" the chipper receptionist asks, when we walk into Theo's office.

"We're here to see Theo," I tell her, hoping she doesn't insist we need an appointment, or worse, he isn't in.

Thankfully, she smiles, then buzzes Theo on the intercom system. "Hey, boss, a couple of ladies are here to see you."

"I'll be right out," he responds.

That was easy. I hope it's a sign our conversation will go as smoothly.

"Hello, ladies! Can I help you with something?" he asks, eyeing the pastry box in my hands which everyone in town recognizes as Juliet's bakery.

"You were at the Red Castle Hotel bar the other night. Right after the celebration of life for Dillon Watkins," I remind him.

"Oh. Yeah," he responds, wincing with embarrassment. "So, we met at the bar?" his eyes dart nervously between Juliet and me like he's worried about what he may have done or said in front of us.

"You were in such awful shape," I continue, "we wanted to stop and check on you. We brought pastries." I offer my best smile, holding the box out. "I tend bar at the hotel, and we talked."

"That's awfully nice of you. Do you do this for all the drunk patrons?"

"Only the ones who happen to live in town," I assure him.

"I didn't know the Red Castle had such great customer service. I should drink there more often."

"You should!"

"Come on back," he says. "We can chat for a bit. You have good timing. I brewed a pot of fresh coffee right before you walked in."

"Great!" Juliet says.

"Someone put me in a cab, right?" he asks, leading us into his office. "Do I owe you cab fare? I'm so embarrassed. I never behave like that."

"The staff at the hotel made sure you got in the cab. And don't worry about the fare. It's on us."

"My memory is a little spotty. I didn't do anything *too* foolish, did I?"

I wave it off like it's no big deal. "You said you killed Dillon Watkins."

"Wow. I was drunk wasn't I? I thought you were going to say I hit on you or something."

"You're pretty calm for someone who learned they confessed to murder," Juliet point out.

"Obviously, I didn't kill him," he laughs. "Dillon had a heart attack. Everyone says so."

"It's not every day I get people confessing to murder in the bar. You also said Dillon was firing you."

"Ouch." He cringes. "I put it all out there, didn't I? It's true, though. Someone told me, Dillon was leaving me. That's probably what confused you. I'm sure I said I *wanted* to kill him."

"No, you said you killed him."

"Okay, okay, I admit it. I was furious with Dillon. But not enough to kill him."

"Why do you think Dillon was firing you?" I felt like I had to tell Mia, Dillon was alive. But I'm not ready to tell Theo yet.

"A friend sent me proof, Dillon was meeting with Jason Duran a fancy agent with a high class firm in New York City."

"Who's the friend?" I ask, frowning at his response. If Dillon lied to me I'll be furious. I'm trying to help him after all.

"I don't know."

"You don't know your friend?" Juliet asks, shaking her head.

"See for yourself," he tells us as he twists his computer monitor toward us showing us an email. The message reads "I saw Dillon Watkins having dinner with Jason Duran at that Italian restaurant under the bridge last night. They look awfully chummy. Rumor has it Dillon is dumping you for him. I thought you should know. Sincerely, A friend."

Dillon swore to me he had no intention of dumping Theo. But clearly this looks like he was. Why would a well paid New York City talent agent take Dillon to dinner just for the heck of it? This picture makes Dillon look like a liar and still doesn't let Theo off the hook.

"You said something else as you were leaving."

"Oh no, I knew it, I did hit on you didn't I?"

"You said Ivan killed Dillon."

"Theo your 10:00 appointment is here," the receptionist tells him over the intercom.

"That settles it. No more tequila shots for this guy. Amiright? I obviously can't hold my liquor," he chuckles uncomfortably. But if you'll excuse me ladies, I have to get back to work. But thank you for the pastries and the interesting conversation."

"Thank you for meeting with us," Juliet tells him, grabbing my arm and sweeping us out the door.

"Why are you being so pushy?" I protest when Juliet practically shoves me out of the office and onto the sidewalk. "You didn't give me a chance to question him about the accusation he made against Ivan."

"You didn't see it?" she asks.

"See what?"

"The green hoodie!"

# Chapter 22

"What green hoodie? Where?"

"I think it was a green hoodie…"

"*Where*?" I shout, stopping so abruptly in the middle of the sidewalk, the couple behind us only narrowly misses running into us.

"Maybe you couldn't see it from where you were sitting, but when he leaned down to pick up the pen he dropped, I swear I saw what looked like a green hoodie sleeve on his chair. Or maybe it was a sweatshirt. I'm not sure. But I know it was green. Wendy told me Mia said she thought someone wearing a green hoodie was following her."

"Yes! It makes perfect sense. Theo wanted to kill Dillon because he thought he was cheating on him with another talent agent. A bigwig from New York City would make him even angrier, I'm sure. Remember, he flat-out confessed to me, but I dismissed it because he was drunk."

"But he also said Ivan killed Dillon," Juliet reminds me.

"Whatever." I respond, quickly dismissing the reminder. "We have to go back and confront him!" I whirl about, heading toward Theo's office, but Juliet grabs *my* arm.

"Are you crazy?" she exclaims.

"No, I'm not crazy. We have a killer to catch." I pause when I realize how ridiculously dangerous it sounds. "Okay, so maybe it isn't the best idea."

"We must tell Sheriff Mack," Juliet pleads.

"C'mon. You and I both know how that will go. 'Hey, Surly Steve, Juliet *thinks* she saw part of a green sweatshirt. Can you bring Theo in for questioning?'"

"Fine." She scowls. "What do you suggest we do? Other than burst into Theo's office demanding to get a better look at the green thing on his chair."

"You go back to the bakery. I'll go back to the gym to question Dillon about the picture."

"Can you trust him?" Juliet asks.

"No. But I still want to know what *he* has to say."

"Dillon!" I whisper on the gym steps, hoping he can hear me. I've had so many one-sided-looking conversations with him in the gym, I fear they're about to ban me. I pause for a moment, but no troublesome ghost. "Dillon!" I whisper again, but a little louder this time.

When a barefoot woman with wet hair, and shoes tucked under her arm, runs from the gym, still buttoning her blouse, and complaining about it being haunted, I know Dillon can't be far behind.

"Heyyyyyy Holly!" he exclaims upon seeing me, with my hands planted on my hips, glaring at him.

"You stay out of the locker rooms!" I scold.

"How did you--" he laughs as he watches the poor woman speed away in her car. "That obvious, huh?"

"You promised me you'd behave while I investigated this case! Stop scaring people."

"Oh, c'mon. Let me have a little fun!" he begs.

"We've already discussed this. I'm working my tail off trying to figure out who killed you, but you keep goofing around."

"Do you know something new?" he gasps.

"Yes! Mia has, er, had, your bottle."

"You found my bottle! Yahoo! I knew you could do it!" he cheers, dancing a happy jig. "Hang on a sec. Mia poisoned me?"

"No. At least, I don't think so. She told us she picked up the bottle after you died. She took it to the chemistry lab at school because she was curious about what made your drink different from the others."

"Did she now? That little scamp. Oh my gosh, you're here to tell me she found poison! I knew it!"

"No, she didn't."

"There's no poison?"

"She couldn't finish testing it."

"Couldn't?" he asks, confusion crossing his face.

"Someone locked her in a closet, then stole the bottle and the sample she was testing."

"It was my killer!"

"It's looking more like it every day."

"I knew it! Is Mia okay? Have you talked to anyone else?" he presses.

"Mia is fine. Shaken, but fine." Truthfully, I'm a little surprised he thought to ask if she was okay. "The Sheriff's Department is keeping an eye on her to be on the safe side. But I mostly came here to tell you Juliet and I met with Theo."

He smiles. Quite fondly. Again, much to my surprise. "How's my old friend doing?"

"Your old friend showed me a picture of you meeting with Jason Duran from New York City. You lied about firing him."

"I swear to you I didn't!" he exclaims, waving his hands about.

"You expect me to believe that some high-powered Manhattan agent just happened to pass through Glenwood Springs, and you just happened to go to dinner with him for no reason?"

His guilt-ridden face confirms it. He's such a liar.

"Okay, okay, I admit it. Duran wanted me to leave Theo--"

"Ha!" I shout before he can continue with his excuse.

"Will you please let me finish?"

"Finish lying?" I snap. Why must these spirits test my patience like this?

"No. Finish the truth. You jump to a lot of conclusions. You should work on that."

"Like you haven't given me a reason!"

"All right. Fair enough. But I swear to you I wasn't leaving Theo. Period. And that's what I told Duran. Theo got me gigs when I started in this business. The days when maybe three students would come to my class, and I had a measly 75 Instagram followers. No one else would even look at me.

"It was Jason Duran who literally laughed in my face the first time I approached him to represent me, not Theo. Duran claimed it was beyond ridiculous that some no-name fitness instructor at a neighborhood gym in a small mountain town would think he needed a rep. Much less a rep like *him* from New York.

"He convinced me he was right, and I'd never amount to anything. The former chubby kid who was so nervous in front of an audience, I almost wet my pants when I had to read a line from a school play. I was ready to quit everything, but Theo stepped in and said he'd do it for next to nothing until I made some money."

"Theo believed in me even when I didn't believe in myself. He got me gigs like advertising for a tire shop in Rifle and a laundromat in Palisade. Before I knew it, I had hundreds of social media followers, and my classes were growing by the day.

"Jason Duran came sniffing around only after the news broke that I had paired up with Ivan on a revolutionary sports drink. He demanded I meet with him and said he'd fly anywhere. I admit it. I only agreed to it because I wanted to laugh in his face when I turned him down.

"Totally immature, but darn if it didn't feel good. The picture Theo showed you had to have been right before I told Duran to get lost. He stormed out of the restaurant he was so angry. By the way, who sent him that picture?"

"He doesn't know. It was sent anonymously and signed by 'a friend,'" I explain.

"I bet it was." He scowls.

"How do I know you aren't telling me a story like you tell Mia and Erica and all the rest of your lady friends?" I press. I admit I'm a little pleased when he looks embarrassed.

"All right, I admit it. I'm horrible about committing to the ladies. But try to look at it from my perspective. I was an overweight, shy guy with bad skin and a cheap haircut. Women never gave me the time of day until I transformed into the adonis you see in front of you."

He only pauses when I roll my eyes so hard I'm surprised I don't hurt myself.

"I'm like a kid in a candy shop. I'm not proud of it, but I have to admit, it's been fun.

"But as for Theo, he's my ride-or-die, man." He halts his speech for a moment while I can practically see the gears turning. "How about this? The restaurant's owner can confirm our fight. He'll tell you how when Duran realized I was leading him on, he screamed at me. Like, screamed at me so bad spit was flying from his mouth. He even flipped his chair over before storming out. It was awesome," he chuckles at the memory. "Come to think of it, isn't it interesting that whoever sent the picture to Theo obviously left that part out."

"That is interesting. But you have to admit this is a pattern with you. You tell me one thing, I go to confirm it and get a different story. I'm doing a lot of back and forth here without results."

"How about this?" he says. "You talk to the restaurant owner today. If he doesn't confirm the public tantrum, I swear I'll go into the light and leave you and everybody else alone."

"Do you mean that? Truly mean that?"

"100%. I know what he'll say, so I'm happy to make the deal." I almost laugh when he holds his hand out as if we can actually shake on it. "It's symbolic." He shrugs.

Symbolic or not, he better mean it because I'm about out of patience.

# Chapter 23

The restaurant opens at 4:00 so I have until then to catch up on some cases I've been neglecting. One of which requires a trip to the library on Cooper Avenue for research. It isn't a big library. It's a small mountain town, after all, but it's big enough for what I need.

I've been hired to investigate spooky occurrences at the local radio station. They believe it's haunted, but don't know why or who it would be. I've visited the station a few times, but so far, no spirits.

Now I'm researching its history to determine if anyone died there and when. I settle into an oversized cushy chair in front of the picture windows to comb through a stack of old newspaper clippings. What I feared would be dull work, considering radio isn't something many of us think about anymore, is surprisingly interesting.

In 1925, the Red Castle Hotel staged a mock radio show, hoping to spark public interest in the new-fangled medium. It was a bust. It wasn't until 1947, that Glenwood finally got its own radio station. Now I need to figure out who, or what, is haunting it.

I'm so engrossed in the research that when I catch just a flash of something green outside, I'm sure I imagined it. But after a few minutes, I see it again. Is that someone in a green hoodie? No. It can't be. I must have green hoodie on the brain. When I look up again, they're gone. I obviously imagined it.

I check my watch and decide I have just enough time to pick up a few more articles to read. But when I stand up and stretch for a moment, a person in a green hoodie ducks behind a shelving cart. What on earth? I can't tell if it's a man or a woman, but it's definitely a green hoodie and I definitely didn't imagine it.

My pulse quickens. Mia swore someone was following her before locking her in the supply closet. Juliet swore she saw something green on Theo's chair. My mind flashes back to our argument about how she insisted we call Sheriff Mack, but I dismissed her. Told her to return to the bakery. What if someone really was after Mia and they saw us talking to her, so now they're after me? Or Juliet? Or Wendy? Why did I have to be so quick to refuse to take this to the Sheriff?

My feet are rooted to the spot. I'm too scared to move. At least I'm in a public place. Whoever it is would be foolish to come after me, wouldn't they? My mind races. What do I do? I could text Sheriff Mack. But what would I tell him? 'Hey, I'm in the library, and I think there's someone here wearing a green hoodie.' He'd be thrilled with that. I could text Juliet or Wendy, but same thing. What could they do? They'll insist I contact the Sheriff.

Before I can call out to the person, whoever they are, they bolt from behind the shelving cart, running across the library.

"No running in the library," a librarian sitting at the checkout desk scolds. Sorry lady, but I have to find out who this is. I drop the articles and run after them.

"Excuse me! I said no running!" the librarian says more forcefully this time. She'll be extra mad when she discovers I dumped old newspaper articles in the middle of the floor.

Hoodie Stalker throws open the front door and sprints across the community plaza. They're fast, but I'm faster. I finally reach whoever it is, stretching my arm out as far as I can. *Yes!* I think when my outstretched hand finally grasps their sleeve.

"What do you think you're doing?" I growl as they turn around to face me. "Erica?"

"Let me go!" she tries to pull her arm back, but I refuse to let her.

"Erica! Why are you following me?" I ask, after she angrily shoves the hood from her head.

"I wasn't following you! I was checking out a book on prenatal care. I didn't realize you were here."

"But your hands are empty. And you ran when I told you not to."

"They didn't have the book I wanted."

"Oh, cut it out. You were following me and Mia, and now you're busted."

"Mia? What are you talking about? I wasn't following Mia!"

"But you were following me."

"Okay, fine! Mia called me to brag about how you're talking to Dillon's ghost, and you're going to let her talk to him as well. I was hoping if I followed you long enough, I would catch you doing it because I have questions for him."

"Did Mia tell you that Dillon's ghost is only at the gym?"

"No! She's such a troll. She didn't tell me that part. Wait. So it's true, though. You *are* talking to Dillon's ghost."

"Yes."

"Has he asked about me? Can I talk to him?" she begs.

"I'll need to ask him first. For the record, I haven't told Mia I'd help her talk to him. I told her I'd think about it."

"Has he asked about me?" she continues to press.

"We've talked about you."

"He's the father of my baby! I demand you take me to him."

"Erica, I know."

"Know what?"

"I know about the paternity test. I know you threw a tantrum in the doctor's office and ripped it up."

Erica hangs her head. "Please, just ask him if he'll talk to me."

"I promise, I will ask." When she walks away I don't know what more to say. I do know I better pick up those newspaper articles from the floor before the librarian comes after me.

"Hi, there. Is the owner in?" I ask the young man working the host desk at La Trattoria Sotto il Ponte.

"Elio?"

"Yes."

"Hang on a sec. I'll get him. Who's asking, by the way?"

"Holly Daniel. I'm a paranormal private investigator," I explain, handing him my card. "I'd like to ask him about the incident that may have occurred here a couple of weeks ago between Dillon Watkins and a man named Jason Duran."

"Oh, yeah, the big show!" he exclaims, his face lighting up. "I wasn't supposed to work that night, but I filled in for a friend who had a date. He's mad he missed it!" He laughs.

"Big show? I heard that Dillon and Jason argued, but I'm not sure I'd call it a big show?" I'm confused. This guy must be talking about someone else.

"It was *so* a big show!"

"All right. Let's start over," I offer, patiently. "I'm talking about two weeks ago. Dillon Watkins, the celebrity fitness trainer, had dinner with Jason Duran, a talent agent from Manhattan. They argued, and Duran stormed out. I'm actually just here to confirm it."

"Oh, it was way more than an argument. I've never seen anyone so mad."

"Which one was mad?" I ask, to be on the safe side.

"The rich guy in the Armani suit. I don't know what Dillon said to set him off, but we almost called the cops."

Well, what do you know? Dillon told the truth for once.

"Everything was fine at first. They were chatting all businesslike until Dillon leaned forward and whispered something. The rich guy screamed at him, jumped to his feet, and threw his chair! I can't believe he didn't hit anybody.

Then he spun around to storm out, but crashed into a server."

The host can barely finish his story he's laughing so hard. In fact, the entire dining room staff stop to listen, nodding and giggling.

"The guy was covered with pasta and marinara!" the tall server with a shaved head chimes in.

"Dude, remember the noodle that was hanging from his ear?" the host adds.

"I laugh every time I think about it!" the bartender exclaims.

"And then a drop of sauce slid down his nose and dripped onto his suit," another server laughs at the memory.

"What about the shrimp sticking out of his pocket?" the busboy guffaws, pointing to his chest.

Okay, this is sad and hilarious.

"Here, check it out. Barney had the best angle," the host explains, showing me a video on his phone.

I admit it's quite funny. Shaved Head server is right. The spaghetti dangling over Duran's ear is hilarious. But I stop laughing when I recognize someone in the background taking pictures.

"Hold on a second. I have to stop the video!" I touch the screen to freeze it. "Let me check something," I explain, expanding the video with my fingers to zero in on the exact face I need.

Just behind Jason, and to his left, filming the entire incident, is none other than Joel Frank.

"You know what's weird, though?" the host says, but it barely registers because I'm obsessed with seeing Joel at the restaurant, holding his phone out as he stands in the perfect spot to take pictures. Pictures he could send to a certain agent.

"Excuse me, miss?" the host says again.

"What? I'm sorry. Did you ask me something?" My mind is so blown by everything that's happened today, I don't know what to think.

"I was going to say when Dillon died, my first thought was Jason Duran did it."

"Whoa! Mine too!" another server says.

My mind is still awhirl, and these guys are talking gibberish? "Did you say you thought Jason killed Dillon?" I ask. I'm sure he didn't just say that.

"I did. At least until they said he had a heart attack."

"Why did you think he killed Dillon in the first place?"

"Because that's what he said right before he left."

"Yeah, man, it was all dramatic and everything. Like a movie," the bald server says. "You stopped the video before the end, so you didn't hear that part."

"Okay." I push play again just in time to watch Jason point at Dillon and shout, "You're dead!"

# Chapter 24

After leaving the restaurant and calling the gym to confirm Joel's teaching schedule, I drive there right away, eager yet nervous, to question him. He must be the one who sent the picture to Theo. I could kick myself for not following up sooner when he joked about killing Dillon.

What if he confessed at the celebration of life without meaning to? A subconscious confession? He *and* Theo confessed to killing Dillon - I don't care if they were drunk or joking or neither, they both said it - and now, the restaurant wait staff has tied them together, which only furthers my suspicions. Why would they say they killed someone who everyone else assumes died from natural causes? Unless they know he didn't?

And, they both think Dillon has threatened their livelihoods. So, that's definitely motive. *But* do they have the ability to poison someone?

This doesn't mean I'm dismissing the others. Not by a long shot. There are still too many loose ends. No matter how much she denies it, Erica could have been the one following Mia. She obviously has a green hoodie and was stalking *me*, so why not Mia? She could have followed her to the lab, locked her in the closet, then stolen the bottle.

But if *she* poisoned Dillon's drink, did she use witchcraft? Would a standard test at the lab have the ability to reveal a spell or lethal potion? I can only imagine Sheriff Mack's response if I asked him about it though.

Assuming we find the bottle, that is. Which is looking less likely by the day. The killer must have disposed of the bottle by now. So, we're relying solely on the ashes to reveal any toxins, and that isn't a sure thing, no matter what kind of poison it might be.

Finally, there's Ivan who knows chemistry, *and* was furious with Dillon for claiming he'd developed the sports drink and then threatened to back out of the marketing efforts.

What a baffling, mixed-up mess this has turned into. *And*, as if I didn't already have enough people who wanted to kill Dillon, now, thanks to the staff at the restaurant, I have another suspect in Jason Duran. After returning to the VW, I searched his name on the internet and located the firm he works for in New York City. The moment I get the chance, I'll call him.

"You're back!" Dillon exclaims. "You went to La Trattoria, didn't you?"

"I did." I nod.

"They confirmed my story, didn't they?"

"They did." I nod again.

"You don't look happy about it, though."

"I need to talk to Joel."

"He's finishing a class. But why him? What does this have to do with you confirming what happened to me at the restaurant?"

"I'll fill you in as soon as I talk to him."

"There he is now!" he points to Joel, who's talking with an older woman in the classroom doorway.

I pause nearby to listen. He's explaining how she can improve her mobility. I notice how patient he is while reviewing the importance of developing a strong core. He tells her it's not about washboard abs, but about having the strength to maintain balance and flexibility. That way, when her grandchildren beg her to play a game with them on the floor, she can do so without worrying about getting up again.

He's so patient and thorough with her. He may not be as adept at promoting himself as Dillon was, but I bet he's a good trainer. He just isn't as flashy as Dillon. It's a shame jealousy may have driven him to murder.

"Excuse me, Joel?" I ask as soon as the woman walks away. Dillon hovers next to me, I wish I could tell him to wait somewhere else.

"Yes?"

"I'm Holly Daniel. We spoke at the celebration of life the other day?"

"Oh, yeah, I remember you. What can I help you with?"

"I have a weird question for you, and I don't know of any other way than to just ask it."

"Okay."

"You were at La Trattoria Sotto il Ponte a couple of weeks ago when Dillon Watkins had dinner with Jason Duran, right?"

The patience he showed with his student vanishes like a wisp of smoke. "I don't know what you're talking about," he snaps. "I've never been there."

"But I saw you there," I insist.

"There must be a mistake. Besides, we only met recently. How would you know it was me?"

"I just do."

"I assure you, you're wrong. Now, if you don't mind, I'm late for a personal training appointment," he insists as he tries to hurry away.

"I have it on video," I call after him. "You're in the background watching Jason and Dillon argue."

Bingo. That got his attention. He stops without turning around. "I'm sorry, but I really am late," he says.

"I know you were there, and I know you took pictures *before* the argument started." Okay, so, I don't know that for sure, but it's a solid prediction.

"Look, lady, I don't know what your game is, but if you don't stop following me, I'll have the manager remove you. Please. Go away."

"I have proof!" I tell him, holding up my phone with the video playing. He may still have his back to me, but the audio from the fight comes out loud and clear.

"Okay, fine, I was there," he declares, spinning on his heel, before closing in on me. I'm startled by his sudden movement, so I pull the phone back while letting the video continue to play. "And I took a few pictures. Big deal. Everyone was taking pictures."

"Yes, everyone was recording the fight. But you took pictures *before* the fight, didn't you?"

"What's your point, lady?"

"My point is, I think you took a picture of Dillon having dinner with Jason, looking oh so cozy, as if they had some sort of secret business arrangement. You then sent the picture to Theo Barlow to convince him Dillon was firing him and switching agents."

"How did you know?" he stammers.

"So, it's true?" Dillon shouts in my ear so loudly it echoes. "You ruined my relationship with Theo, and I never had a chance to explain what really happened!" he screams angrily.

When he rises, pausing in mid-air, it's like time stops, and everything is eerily quiet for a moment. I know exactly what he's about to do, and even though I scream at him not to, he throws himself at Joel, passing through him and imposes an other-wordly infusion in a harsh way.

As a spirit communicator, I've only experienced it once, and to describe it as unpleasant doesn't begin to cover it. I at least knew what was happening. A person who had little knowledge of spirits or worse, didn't realize they exist would be terrified.

When it happened to me it was as if my body was plunged into ice water, despite it being a sweltering August afternoon. My hair stood on end while my insides felt like they were being electrically charged. I imagine it's what it feels like right before being struck by lightning. After that, my limbs were like cement had weighed them down and I fell to the ground.

Clara tells me it's quite rude and not something any self-respecting ghost does.

After Dillon passes through Joel, his face is ashen. He clutches the wall for support as he sways. Fearing he's about to vomit on my shoes, I back up.

"What did you do to me?" he screams. "Are you a witch?"

"No, of course not! I didn't do anything!"

A small crowd gathers to watch us argue. It's not how I expected this to go at all. They can tell something is going on, but they don't understand what. They don't know why Joel is screaming at me.

When Joel lurches toward me, his steps shaky but determined, Dillon passes through him a second time. He falls to the ground screaming in fear.

After that, Dillon loses control. Everything that's small enough for him to knock down, he does. He knocks over plants, kicks a nearby volleyball, and pushes over a display stand holding fliers and brochures advertising classes and services the gym offers. As a new ghost, his strength is limited, but his rage is giving him power. If something is too heavy to push over, he makes it sway it instead. He flies around the gym doing this to everything he can.

People are no longer interested in the argument between Joel and me. Instead, they're watching things rock back and forth or crash to the ground. Now they're scared.

Bob storms from his office. "What is going on here?"

Dillon takes to throwing things at Joel. Pens, paper, and even a squash ball he's snatched from someone's hand. The man is so frightened he leaps up and sprints from the building.

"Stop it!" I shout at Dillon. "Stop it right now!"

"I never touched you!" Joel cries as he cowers on the ground, not understanding what's happening to him.

"Not you! It's D--" I freeze. This is not the time to admit I see dead people.

"It's her! She's a witch! She's doing this!" he points at me.

Thankfully, for my sake, no one is listening. They're all running for safety, dropping towels, water bottles, weights, and whatever else they're holding before fleeing the gym in droves.

Just when I think it can't get any worse, Dillon somehow sets off the indoor sprinkler system. Water rains down on all, while more members flee.

"Out! Out! Please, everyone! This way!" Bob tries desperately to herd the remaining gym members outside.

Dillon's ghost conveniently disappears. "Coward!" I call out while heading for the door.

With the gym finally empty, we all gather in the parking lot, waiting for the Glenwood Springs Fire Department to shut down the sprinklers. We mill about soaking wet and miserable, while staring up at the gym, with water dripping everywhere. A mixture of horror and confusion shows on most people's faces. But on my face, it's anger.

Not only has Dillon failed to keep up his end of our agreement, but he may also have cost a man his business.

# Chapter 25

**C**ome to the bakery **NOW. 911!**

Is how the text from Juliet, that's buzzing my phone at the crack of dawn, reads.

I fumble with the phone, only to drop it on the hardwood floor, resulting in an obnoxiously loud clatter. Of course, it had to completely miss the plush, colorful throw rug next to the bed.

"Keep it down over there. I'm trying to sleep," Mystery mumbles from the chair in front of the window. Why a ghost cat needs sleep, I'm not sure. But otherworldly or not, she is a cat, after all.

I attempt to shake the grogginess from my head, leap out of bed, and nearly trip and fall I'm so freaked out. This isn't how I planned to wake up this morning.

Especially after the way yesterday's trip to the gym ended. Bob was forced to close the gym until further notice and I blame myself. Yes, Dillon's the one who went off the rails, destroying and damaging everything he could, in addition to scaring all the members away. If only I had confronted Joel elsewhere, none of it would have happened.

Now it's Juliet who's in trouble. What if someone robbed the bakery? What if she's bleeding to death? Okay, so that probably isn't the case. I doubt she'd be able to text us if it were. But even if she isn't bleeding to death, I'm terrified. I tried calling, but she won't pick up. What if whoever killed Dillon knows we're investigating this and did something to her?

Just as I pull up in front of the bakery, Wendy also screeches to a stop on her mint green Vespa. She must have driven like a woman possessed. Who knew those things could move so fast?

"What's going on?" I cry, leaping from the VW while we scramble toward the door.

"I don't know!" Wendy exclaims.

What if it's locked? How will we get in? Can Wendy open it with magic? What happens if we find Juliet passed out on the floor of the bakery? Should I have called 911 before we got here? The worst possible scenarios race through my mind. Robber? Mountain lion? Flood? Fire? I can't stop them from overwhelming my imagination.

Thankfully, we don't need magic because the door is indeed unlocked. Wendy flings it open before we both sprint inside, only to find Juliet sitting in a chair sipping coffee.

"You're drinking coffee?" Wendy shrieks with disbelief.

"Where's the emergency?" I beg.

"I desperately needed coffee," she says, nodding at a lump on the table next to her.

The lump is a green hoodie. The one Erica was wearing while spying on me yesterday. Actually, I don't know. It *looks* the same. But it is just a plain green hoodie, so I can't be certain.

"Before you ask," she says, staring at me, "I can't tell if it's the same one from Theo's office."

Drat. It figures.

She continues. "I took a stack of boxes out to recycling, like I do every morning, but when I opened the lid on the dumpster, this was lying on top."

Wendy and I stare at it like it might jump up and bite us.

"Look inside," she says as if she's reading my mind. "But don't touch anything."

Wendy and I turn to each other. "Go ahead," I tell her.

"You go ahead," she insists.

"I don't want to go ahead."

What if there's a baby inside? But wouldn't it move? What if it's an animal? An injured animal? I can't handle this. Juliet would never spring something like that on us, right? Of course not! I'm still freaking out. I can't touch it.

Juliet groans when Wendy and I refuse to move. "Oh, for the love of sam, I'll do it!" she exclaims before pulling the hoodie back.

Then Wendy screams. I throw my hand over my mouth to keep from screaming. It's a sport bottle. With the name "Dillon" written across the side.

"This was in the recycling bin?" Wendy whispers.

"Yes, it was." When Wendy finally steps forward, Juliet thrusts her hand out to stop her. "Don't touch it! There might be fingerprints."

"Oh. Yeah. Of course." Wendy nods nervously.

"Have you called Sheriff Mack?" I ask.

"I was waiting for you," she explains.

"We have to call him," I tell her, my voice shaking.

"I agree," Wendy says with an equally shaky voice while Juliet nods.

Following a vigorous round of rock, paper, scissors, of course I lose and have to be the one to call him. While the phone rings I cross as many fingers as I can hoping he's already awake and had his coffee along with a hearty breakfast. My hopes are dashed when he answers with a garbled, "Mack here."

After I tell him what we found, he hangs up. I'm assuming that means he's on his way.

"I need coffee!" I announce.

"I need sugar!" Wendy says.

"Help yourselves," Juliet tells us, refusing to move from the chair she's been sitting in since we arrived. She hasn't taken her eyes off the bundle.

"I really wish you hadn't touched this," Sheriff Mack says after Juliet explains what happened. He's wearing a t-shirt and jeans, and I barely recognize him. I've only seen him in uniform or dress clothes. Clara would swoon for sure. She loves to flirt with him, although he doesn't know of course.

Juliet taps her foot in annoyance. "I didn't know what it was until after I touched it. It didn't even occur to me that it must be *the* hoodie until I started to pick it up, and Dillon's bottle fell out."

"Why did you pick up a hoodie left in the trash, to begin with?" he complains.

"Because it was a bright green hoodie in the recycle bin sitting on top of boxes. It seemed out of place, so I picked it up. But when I did, the bottle fell out."

"Please tell me you didn't touch the bottle," he groans.

"Of course not. I picked it up very carefully using the sweatshirt, brought it in here, and texted these two in a panic."

"Why would someone put it in the recycle bin?" I ask.

"I bet they thought it was regular trash," Sheriff Mack says.

"But they put it in Juliet's bin. What if they're targeting her? She could be in danger," I insist.

Juliet shakes her head. "All the businesses along this block use that container," she says, making a sweeping motion with her hand to indicate it's a lot. "If you're one of those businesses, you'd know. Otherwise, you wouldn't."

"If someone was targeting Juliet, they would have left it closer to the bakery. Like on the doorstep. I'll have a deputy check the area out to be sure, but I doubt we'll find anything."

"Are there any cameras in the area?" I ask.

"I don't think so. But you'll have to ask the others nearby. We've never had trouble, so I don't think anyone has bothered," Juliet explains.

"I have to tell you something," I mumble in the Sheriff's direction.

"What?" he throws his hands up in irritation.

Shouldn't he be used to this by now?

"I caught Erica following me around yesterday. She was wearing a green hoodie."

"What?" Juliet and Wendy exclaim in stereo.

"When were you going to tell me?" Sheriff Mack asks.

"Soon? Ish? Soonish!" I insist. "Things got hectic yesterday."

"We might as well tell him about the other thing," Juliet says.

"Why doesn't this surprise me?" he asks, rubbing his hand over his short, blunt haircut.

"I think I saw the sleeve of a green hoodie, or maybe a sweatshirt on Theo's chair when we went to see him," Juliet squeaks.

"What did he say?" he sighs.

"Let's just say I have a lot to catch you up on," I tell him.

"Wonderful. Is it urgent?" he asks in a way that tells me he doesn't think this is wonderful at all.

"I can write it all down for you if you want."

"That would be best. In the meantime, I'll have the bottle taken to the lab that has the cremains and ask them to expedite testing for both," he says. "Someone clearly didn't want themselves connected to the bottle and went out of their way to dispose of it."

"We finally have a breakthrough in this case, ladies!" I declare with relief. "And gentleman," I add quickly when the Sheriff raises an eyebrow at me. "This is so encouraging. We'll finally have answers about the poison."

"Assuming it's poison," the Sheriff reminds me.

"If it wasn't poisoned, why would they bother to dispose of the bottle like that?"

"Fair enough," he nods.

"If I was going to dispose of evidence, I'd take it down to the river," Wendy tells us.

"Duly noted," Sheriff Mack says, pretending to make a note of what Wendy said and trying not to smile.

"Sheriff Mack, did you make a joke?" Juliet teases.

"Don't you mean Surly Steve?" he asks before turning on his heel and walking out of the bakery, leaving us to stare after him in shock.

"How did he know?" Wendy mouths.

# Chapter 26



*Two Days Later*

**T**he toxicology tests are in. I need to see you in person, but not at the station.** Sheriff Mack texts.

Oh, happy day; we're finally getting somewhere. I had a good feeling about this when I woke up this morning. After the disaster at the gym, I'm eager to wrap this up and move on. It's about time we got some answers.

**I just brewed a fresh pot of coffee. Come on over! Clara will be glad to see you.**

**K**

Uh oh. That's not a good sign. Why wouldn't he just tell me over the phone? What's up with the secrecy? Is it worse than I imagined? Who could it point to? What if it's a serial killer? As usual, my imagination leaps down the rabbit hole of worst-case scenarios.

I sent Sheriff Mack a lengthy email after leaving the bakery the other day, explaining everything I'd learned since we last spoke because I already knew he'd insist on a written report. The only thing I haven't updated him on yet is my conversation with the office manager in Jason Duran's office. She told me that Mr. Duran was out of the country when Dillon died, so that automatically rules him out.

"He's here! He's here!" Clara cheers when the doorbell rings.

"Who invited the fuzz?" Mystery exclaims, running to hide as usual before I can get to the door. What kind of life did that cat lead when she was alive that she's so nervous around the authorities? Was she a cat burglar? I've scolded her about not calling the Sheriff inappropriate names, but my lecturing has obviously gone ignored. "You shouldn't say things like that!" I tell her anyway before opening the door.

"Welcome, Sheriff," I tell him as he steps inside. Despite his sour mood, I'm excited we'll finally learn what really killed Dillon. Of course, I've had my theories all along, but now we have facts.

"I can't stay long," he grunts.

Oh, goody. His mood still hasn't changed.

"No problem. Lay it on me," I tell him, showing him the warmest smile possible, hoping it will melt his icy demeanor. "What did the tests show? Arsenic? Cyanide? Ricin?" Yes, I've done my research. Imagine what the authorities would say if, for some reason, they ever had to examine my internet search history!

"The reports came back negative for any toxins," he says without fanfare. "Everything is completely safe. Not a poison in sight."

I stare at him in stunned silence. The enormous clock that hangs in the hallway ticks down the moments. I can't tell if it's seconds or even minutes before I react. "How can that be?" I cry. After everything we've been through, I was sure at least one of the tests would confirm poison.

Has this all been nothing but a joke? Has Dillon been scamming me the whole time? Was I a fool to trust him? His destructive tantrum at the gym the other day made me doubt his sincerity, but I refused to think about it until after we got the test results. And here we are, with negative tests.

When we were waiting in the parking lot for the fire department, Bob told me plans to close the gym permanently. When I tried to talk him into making it temporary, he shook his head and mumbled how horrible his luck has been lately, so why bother? I considered telling him about Dillon's spirit and the deal I made with him, but I held off because I was sure we'd have answers soon. But the answers tell us the whole thing has been nothing but a lie?

"I can't believe there's no poison." I bury my head in my hands, biting back tears. "Wait!" I exclaim. "What about fingerprints? There have to be fingerprints on the bottle!"

"The only finger prints belong to Dillon and Mia," he says plainly.

He's never sounded so cold. Am I the worst private investigator ever, or what? I made a deal with a ghost who has been scamming me this whole time. Why am I such a fool?

"It gets better," Sheriff Mack snaps. Poor Clara stands nearby wringing her hands, looking like she isn't sure what to do. If she weren't a ghost, she'd probably cry too. "Dillon's parents are suing the department for emotional distress."

"They can't do that!" I insist. "Can they?"

"We seized their son's cremains and refused to return them until we tested them. All with baseless claims which I can't even explain to my superiors, much less the public, unless I want to face a recall election in the fall."

"Tell them it's my fault. I'll take full blame for everything," I demand.

"And how am I going to do that? Hey Mr. and Mrs. Watkins, so sorry about your son. We seized his ashes from the post office and refused to return them until we ran a bunch of tests because the town ghost whisperer said your son's spirit told her to."

"Maybe you could re-run them to make sure? There has to be a mistake. I've been thinking if Erica was the killer and she used witchcraft, it wouldn't appear in normal tests, right? Is there anyone in the forensics lab who will check for witchcraft?" As soon as that entire speech leaves my mouth, I regret it.

"That's your answer?" he yells. "Oopsie, let's run more tests because a ghost who was a spoiled brat in real life wants us to think he was murdered?"

"You don't have to be mean about it," I pout.

"Mean? Mean? Holly, I am in so much trouble right now with the county commissioners, I can scarcely believe it. I'm prohibited from talking to Dillon's parents or having anything to do with this case ever again. If they knew I was here telling you about the test results..." He stops short, running his hand down his face. "They're talking about suspending me or even censuring me. I've never gotten so much as a rip, and now I'm looking at serious repercussions that would affect my entire career."

Gulp. He never calls me Holly. It's always Ms. Daniel. "I'm so sorry. Is there anything I can do?" I squeak as a tear slides down my cheek. I wipe it away angrily. Dangit. I promised myself I wouldn't cry.

"Just leave me alone," he says. "And stop dragging me into your cases. Dillon Watkins died from natural causes. The end."

With that, he flings open the door and stomps down the walkway without so much as a glance back.

I should have insisted Dillon go into the light the first time he appeared. The medical examiner said it was just a heart attack, so who do I think I am? Like, somehow, I know better than a medical doctor?

If I hadn't made the ridiculous deal with Dillon in the first place, Bob's gym would still be operating as usual, and the Sheriff wouldn't be in trouble at work. I'm a failure, and I drag other people down with me.

I stomp outside to the garage and grab a shovel because it's the only thing I can think of to keep from completely losing it. I created a beautiful garden here to help manage stress. I was convinced it was making me a softer, more likable person.

For what? So I can take the word of an obnoxious ghost? So I can torment his poor parents? So I can get Sheriff Mack censured or, worse, thrown out of office? So I can cost a small business owner his livelihood?

I thrust the shovel into the earth, prepared to dig up the first rose bush. Every last piece of this garden is going where it belongs. In the trash.

But I can't. Despite how mad I am; I can't destroy all this beauty. The old me would have. The old me would have piled it high and lit it on fire.

But I need to do something, so I decide to dig up several large, dead bushes. I've been putting it off since I moved here. For hours, I attack the horrendous things that I've been planning to take out from day one, but never seem to have the time. They're big and ugly and prickly and messy and I hated them from the beginning. I work nonstop. I don't even pause to drink water.

By the time I'm done, I'm a sweaty, dirty, scratched-up mess, but much to my surprise, I actually feel a little better. Don't get me wrong. I still feel horrible that I've caused so many people so much pain, but instead of purposely causing more, I realize I need to think this through.

Although though the gym is closed, I have to talk to Dillon. I have to tell him he wasn't poisoned. *I* did what *I* was supposed to do. Now he can live up to his part of the agreement. It's time for him to cross over.

Then maybe I can convince Bob to file a claim with the insurance company, put the gym back together, and reopen it. Who knows? Maybe I'll tell him about Dillon. It's worth a shot, at least. I'd like to help get somebody out of this disaster.

# Chapter 27

I'm so determined to set things right - well, as right as I can - I seriously consider going to the gym as is, despite my absurdly messy appearance. Considering I'm only talking to a ghost, who cares? But eventually, I realize a long, scalding hot shower would also help my emotional state. And it does!

As much as the old me wants to hide away from the world for as long as I can, the new me remembers I have friends I can rely on. I text Juliet and Wendy to update them, telling them I need to lie low and decompress for a couple of days.

I also tell them we're not to bother Sheriff Mack under any circumstances. I still don't know how to make it right for him, so perhaps the best thing to do, for now anyway, is to leave him alone.

I would also like to contact Dillon's parents to apologize, but I worry it will trace back to the Sheriff, and I've already done more than enough damage there.

For now, I'll focus on doing what only *I* can do and communicate with the unruly gym spirit to convince him to cross over.

I try to avoid looking at the neon red sign on the gym door which reads CLOSED UNTIL FURTHER NOTICE. It hurts my heart too much. Bob must be devastated.

"You broke our agreement," I scold Dillon when he appears on the gym steps.

"I know," he sighs. "I just got so mad that Joel betrayed me in such a petty way. All it did was hurt Bob, who was never anything but amazing to me. Hey, wait a second. Did the test results come back? Is that why you're here? Or is it to yell at me? Which, I admit, I totally deserve. But when they confirm I was poisoned, we can figure out who did it and Bob can re-open the gym!"

Is he seriously sticking with this convoluted story? "You weren't murdered," I tell him in a not-so-gentle way. I'm tired of his antics.

"But of course I was. The tests will prove it. We have to be patient."

"The forensics lab tested your ashes along with the bottle's contents—"

"—you found my bottle?" he cuts me off.

"It was dumped in a recycle bin."

"So, test it!"

"I was getting to that. Like I said, the lab examined both your cremains and the bottle's contents and they didn't find a single toxin."

"That's impossible!" he exclaims. "They're wrong. Tell them to re-test everything!"

"I suggested that."

"And?" he asks hopefully.

"It didn't go over well. Those tests are highly accurate. If they say no poison, then no poison. And to make things worse--"

"It gets worse?"

"Yes. Sheriff Mack is in trouble because I insisted you were poisoned, and I demanded he test everything. He may lose his job!"

"Oh man, that stinks."

"And--"

"There's more?" he groans.

"There's more. Your parents are suing the Sheriff's Department for emotional distress."

He looks so deflated I almost feel sorry for him. I'm still angry with him for trashing the gym, but his disappointment feels genuine. "In a way, it's good, right?" he says.

"How is this good?" I ask.

"No one hated me enough to murder me."

Oh. He has a point. Now I feel even worse.

"I just dropped dead from a random heart attack." He shrugs. "You don't think it will affect sales of Ivan's drink, do you? You have to make sure everyone knows it was a heart attack and had nothing to do with the new drink. I've been thinking about it lately, and I'd feel horrible if it hurt his business."

"That's actually very nice of you to consider."

"Yeah, yeah, I can be an immature jerk. I admit it. But sometimes I'm not so bad!"

"Sometimes." I smile. "By the way, what's the name of the drink? I don't think you ever told me."

"We never settled on a name. Yet another thing we were always arguing about."

"I don't get it," I sigh. "I was sure whoever locked Mia in the closet and then dumped the bottle, did it because they poisoned the drink. Why bother otherwise? It makes no sense."

"You're positive *she* didn't find any toxins?"

"They locked her in the closet before she finished."

"I'm curious, what did she find before she got interrupted? I'm kind of impressed she could do that. We never really talked. Or maybe she talked, but I didn't listen."

"No doubt." I bite my tongue to keep from saying something rude. I pull the list from my pocket, which I've been carrying like some sort of talisman. I kept it to remind myself why we were doing this. Hoping somehow it would magically reveal a clue. Fat chance of that.

"She found cherry flavoring--" I read.

"Ah yes, cherry was my favorite."

"Red 40 food coloring, egg, water--"

"Hang on!" Dillon throws up his hand. "Egg?"

"Yeah, I thought it was weird too, but you obviously know better than I do what was in the drink. Was it for extra protein?"

"Mia is mistaken. I promise you; there are no eggs in our drink."

"That's what she found." I wave the paper in front of him.

"I *know* the drink doesn't have eggs because I'm allergic to them! Like deathly allergic."

I glance at his wrist, looking for the medical alert bracelet people wear when they have life-threatening allergies. But he doesn't have one. One of my foster moms was allergic to nuts, so she wore a bracelet in case something happened, the hospital would adjust their treatment.

"But you don't have a medical alert bracelet."

"Those are for sissies. And it clashed with my outfits," he laughs.

"But you would get sick if you ate eggs, wouldn't you?"

"Lady. I could *die* from eating eggs."

"Could you have a heart attack?"

"Yes!"

We stare at each other in shock. Then it hits me.

"Did anyone else know you were allergic?"

"Aside from my doctor and my parents?"

"Obviously."

"Ivan knew."

# Chapter 28

"Everybody buckled in?" I ask after we stop at Sol Conceptions Bakery to pick up Juliet.

"Aye! Aye! Captain!" Wendy exclaims.

"This is so exciting!" Clara squeals from the back seat of the VW bus.

Shortly before leaving the gym - Dillon was incredibly disappointed he couldn't come along - I texted Juliet and Wendy with a game plan. And yes, I tried to give Dillon a ride in the bus, but it didn't work. The moment I drove off the lot, he disappeared from the passenger seat, only to reappear on the gym steps. We tried several times, but it was useless.

I promised him I would relay everything that happens though. After witnessing his disappointment, I knew I had to go home and pick up Mystery and Clara, who, for some reason, *can* ride in the VW.

Next, we picked up Wendy at the bookstore and then Juliet. Of course, they were happy to help after I filled them in on Dillon's confession. I assured them they didn't have to, but they wouldn't hear of staying out of it.

"One for all and all for one!" Wendy declares.

"I still say we should let Sheriff Mack know," Juliet urges. No surprise there. Always the cautious one.

"Absolutely not," I tell her. "Think of a time when you're sure he was the maddest he's ever been with me—"

"—that time you accidentally dropped his new phone down the sewer grate?" Juliet offers.

"Oh, no, I've got a better one," Wendy laughs. "Remember the time she backed into the mailbox at the Sheriff's Department, in front of the Governor, during his birthday party?"

"That was kind of a rhetorical question," I point out in irritation. "But anyway, he's way madder now."

Clara nods. "I was there. I saw it."

"Clara just backed me up, by the way," I explain. "The scary part is, it isn't so much that he's mad at me. He's mad at himself. He's also scared and worried. He could lose his job, you guys. Between the three of us, I'm pretty sure we can take Ivan if we have to. Juliet and Wendy, I trust you can use magic if things get dicey?"

They nod enthusiastically. Outstanding. We're all set.

"What if he has a big gun?" Mystery asks.

"Thank you for that, Mystery; that's very helpful," I tell her.

We arrive at Ivan's office and, at Clara's insistence, park directly in front of the building, in the loading zone. "That way, I might catch some of the action," she explains.

She's not wrong to anticipate it. She was with me the time we chased a bad guy in the bus *and* the time we were taken hostage, also in the bus, but by a different bad guy. I may have caused Sheriff Mack more grief than he bargained for since I moved here, but Clara says it's the most exciting year of her life. Or her afterlife, as it were.

"We'll stop for a catpuccino afterward, right?" Mystery asks.

"Yes, please!" Clara sings, clapping her hands. "In the drive-through!"

"I suppose," I groan.

"What did they ask for?" Wendy says, laughing.

"They want to visit the coffee shop drive-through after we catch the bad guys," I tell her, shaking my head in disbelief.

"Oh, I want a sweet cream cold brew," Juliet says.

"Woo hoo!" Clara shouts.

"Fine. We'll hit the coffee shop afterward. But can we please focus on catching the bad guy for now?"

When we march into Ivan's office, given the way everyone is staring at us, we must be quite the sight. I have yet to figure out how we'll approach him. But, thankfully I don't have to worry about it because he's already in the lobby, near the door, talking to a tall man in a suit.

"Ivan Moss, we know you murdered Dillon Watkins," I announce loudly, bringing the entire shared office space to a shocked standstill.

"Yes, we mean you," Wendy says when he stares at us, in shock.

He's obviously wondering how we figured it out.

"Call security," he tells the receptionist, who quickly obliges.

"Yes, security should hear this," I tell him.

"What on earth are you talking about?"

"You murdered Dillon, and we can prove it," Juliet says.

"You said that already, but I don't know what you're talking about. Dillon had a heart attack. Everyone knows that."

"After he died, a chemist named Mia Nunez took Dillon's sports bottle. The one he drank from right before he died."

I was sure that would get him, but he doesn't flinch. Fine. This guy is a tough nut.

"She wanted to see what was in the drink you developed. What made it so special," Juliet explains.

"Okay." He shrugs.

Man, this guy is cold.

"She found eggs in it," I tell him.

He laughs. "Well, this chemist of yours isn't much of a chemist, because I guarantee there are no eggs in our drink. Dillon was allergic. He's been allergic the entire time I've known him, which is forever, as you already know. I took great pains to make sure the drink was processed in a facility that was 100% egg free."

When the security officers arrive, moving toward our group, Ivan stops them. "Hold up, guys."

"You slipped what I'm assuming is powdered egg into Dillon's drink because you'd had it with his antics and his threats to withdraw his support. Believe me, I get it. He's a pill. But it's no reason to kill him."

"I can't believe you're telling me you think Dillon was murdered."

"I know he was," I insist.

"And you think I did it because I knew about his egg allergy?"

"Yes. He swears no one else knew," Wendy says.

"But I was in Aspen for two days meeting with investors when Dillon died," Ivan explains patiently.

"You have proof of this?"

"Of course."

"So, pretending you're telling the truth, who else would have known?" I press.

"How am I supposed to kn-- oh no." He pales, reaching for a chair that isn't there. A security guard grabs one nearby and helps him sit.

"What is it?" I demand.

"I told Theo Barlow," he says, his voice becoming a hoarse whisper.

"Why would you tell Theo?" Wendy asks.

"We were at a fitness expo in San Diego last year, where we watched Dillon flit from woman to woman all weekend. We ended up at a pub together drinking beer; next thing you know, we're letting off steam and complaining about how hard it is to be friends with Dillon at times. I told him he'd be surprised to know Dillon is so vain he refuses to tell anyone he's allergic to eggs. We had a good laugh, and I didn't think about it again."

My stomach flip flops at the news. "This is very important, so I need you to think carefully," I say it slowly. "Did you tell anyone else?"

"No! Of course not. I mean, who cares about his allergies?"

"I think Theo did."

"I swear, I've never had that conversation with anyone else," he insists.

"Okay, ladies, we have to find Theo," I tell them.

"Why am I not surprised?" Juliet says.

"Wait! Wait!" Ivan shouts, chasing after us as we head for the door.

What now?

"I think Erica knew?" he says breathlessly.

"When I met you, you claimed you didn't know Erica," I remind him.

"I didn't. I mean, I didn't *realize* I knew her. After you asked me about it, though, I got curious and had my legal team check into it, in case she made trouble for us later. When they showed me a picture, I realized she went to brunch with us once. She was the girl of the day," I suppose.

"If you barely knew her, why would you tell her about Dillon's egg allergy?"

"I didn't tell her. She was being all lovey-dovey and tried to feed him a bite of her asparagus quiche. He wasn't paying attention because he was so busy talking about himself and nearly ate what she was holding in front of him. When he realized what it was, he shot back so fast his chair flew out from under him, and he tumbled to the ground. When Erica asked him what was wrong, he claimed he saw a spider on his plate. He thought, somehow, the egg allergy made him look weak. But I saw the look on her face. I'm sure she knows."

"We have to call Sheriff Mack," Juliet insists again as we make our way out to the bus.

"No. Not yet," I reply. "Not until we're sure. If Ivan is telling the truth, it could be Erica *or* Theo. Erica's hair salon is up the street. Let's confront her there because it's in a public place. Hopefully, if she tries to curse us, you could hold her off, right?"

"I think so," Wendy says.

Not the enthusiastic response I was hoping for, but I'll take it.

"Where's the bad guy?" Mystery asks as we climb back into the bus.

"We haven't found him yet," I explain.

"So, next stop is the coffee shop?"

"Not yet!" I snap.

"You don't have to be cranky about it." Mystery sticks her tongue out at me.

"Hold on a second!" I exclaim as I start to pull away from the curb, hitting the brakes instead. Mystery falls off the backseat, grumbling about how I don't pay her enough for this. "Assuming it's either Theo or Erica who laced Dillon's drink with eggs, and that's the reason they stole the bottle from Mia in the first place, they would have to assume she discovered the eggs."

"Mia doesn't know the eggs are poison to Dillon," Wendy points out.

"But she could be in danger and not realize it," I explain.

"You better call her," Juliet pleads.

"Good thinking." I press call on the phone. "C'mon, c'mon, pick up!" I mumble when it rings endlessly. "Mia! It's Holly!" I exclaim with relief when she finally answers.

"Oh, hey, what's up?"

"I have to tell you something. Where are you?"

"I'm at sch--"

The last thing I hear before the call cuts off is a blood-curdling scream.

# Chapter 29

"Mia! Mia!" I shout at the dead phone.

"What happened?" Juliet asks.

"She screamed, and the line went dead."

"Did she say where she was?" Wendy asks.

"Sch."

"Sch? What's sch?" Clara says.

"School?" Juliet offers.

"The chemistry lab!" Wendy shouts. "Let's go!"

The race to the campus is excruciating. I keep hoping Mia saw a mouse or a grasshopper running across the lab floor, and she'll call me laughing and embarrassed about screaming. But the closer we get to campus, the more I realize, there was no critter. Something horrible has happened.

When we arrive at the school, I panic-park on the sidewalk nearest to the science building. It's as close as I can manage without driving across the lawn and through the quad. But you can bet I considered doing just that. I urge

Clara and Mystery to guard the VW. I don't want to get towed, but Mia's safety is more important.

"What do I do if someone tries to tow us?" Clara asks.

"I don't know. Lean on the horn or something. Maybe that will hold them off."

"Should we split up to look for them?" Wendy asks.

"No, if either Theo or Erica is there, it will be safer as a group," I insist.

"What if they've already taken off?" Juliet worries.

"I don't know. We'll figure it out when we get there. I have to assume she's in the chemistry lab again."

"But what about all those doors? How will we know which lab she's in?" Wendy cries.

"I don't know!" I bark at her. This is horrible. Why didn't we think to warn Mia earlier?

Then I see him. "Look!" I shout, pointing as he waves us down from across the quad.

"Look at what?" Wendy asks.

"Oh. Right. Never mind. The ghost with the head injury I saw last time we were here is waving at us. He must know where they are."

"Room 37!" he shouts as we draw closer. "They're in the basement! Hurry!"

It occurs to me at that point, we don't have a weapon of any kind aside from witchcraft. If it's Erica, I hope that

Wendy and Juliet are more powerful than she is. I recall the rash she gave Mia and shudder. Imagine what she's capable of when she's cornered?

I pause at a fire extinguisher hanging on the wall. It should do the trick.

"What are you doing?" Juliet exclaims when I pull it down.

"Weapon!" I shout while we resume our frenzied scramble to room 37.

The door is closed but Wendy yells *aperire!* magically flinging it open with a huge crash.

We pause in shock when we discover Theo Barlow attempting to strangle Mia. Fortunately, our shock is short lived. "We're here Mia!" I shout, as I strike Theo across the back with the fire extinguisher while Juliet grabs a heavy janitor's broom hitting him dead center in the face. It's enough to momentarily stun him. Mia recovers quickly as the four of us jump on him, forcing him to the ground. He's surprisingly strong, and I don't know how long we can hold him down. He can't escape. I won't let him.

"There's duct tape next to the door!" Mia shouts.

I jump up, grab the duct tape, and run back. It's a struggle involving a lot of biting and scratching and a solid right cross from Wendy, but we finally secure his arms and legs. Enough that he isn't going anywhere for now.

"Go ahead Wendy. Curse him!" I shout.

Wendy looks at me like I've lost my mind until Juliet elbows her. When she realizes what I'm up to, she raises her arms, and sings what I'm pretty sure is gibberish, as if she's winding up to curse him.

"No! Please no!" he cries.

"Start talking! You put eggs in Dillon Watkins' drink didn't you?" I exclaim.

"I don't know what you're talking about!" he insists.

We jump in surprise when Juliet utters a real curse to blow up a glass beaker nearby before turning to Theo, pretending to be ready to do the same to him.

"All right! All right! Don't hurt me! I was so sure when I saw the picture of Dillon with Jason Duran that he was leaving me. I mean why wouldn't he? A high-class, fancy Manhattan talent agent responsible for making some of the biggest names in the fitness business rich? Of course he was leaving me!

"Besides, I knew what a player he was. He had a girl for practically every day of the week, and whenever one of them found out, he still convinced them he'd never do it again. I assumed he'd do it to me, too. He was pretty much my only client. Without him, I was out of a job."

"So, you thought murder was the proper response?" I ask.

"No! Of course not! I never intended to kill him, but when I remembered Ivan telling me Dillon was allergic to eggs, I thought, here's my chance. I'll make him sick. Embarrass him a little. Maybe the New York agent would think he was in bad shape and dump him. I'd be there to pick up the pieces, of course. I never meant to kill him. But who could imagine that something like a little egg allergy would kill someone?"

When I gasp out loud everyone turns to look at me. "That's why you said Ivan killed Dillon."

"I honestly don't remember that. I was drunk after all. I'm telling you, he wasn't supposed to die! My Aunt Irene is allergic to shellfish," he continues to tell his tale. "If she's accidentally exposed to it, she breaks out in huge hives, goes to the urgent care, and gets a shot. That's it. I assumed that's how Dillon would react. A popular fitness expert breaks out in hives during class, and someone has to rush him to the doctor. It never occurred to me he'd keel over from a heart attack!"

"Why didn't you come forward right away?" Wendy asks. "You could have made a better case for it being an accident. After waiting and covering it all up, it made it far worse."

"I considered it. But when the medical examiner said it was a heart attack, I thought it was a sign."

"A sign that you'd gotten away with it!" Mia growls while Theo shrugs sheepishly.

"No doubt," I respond. "But why go after Mia if you thought you got away with it?"

"After the excitement died down and the paramedics left, I tried to get the bottle, but I saw her," he nods at Mia. "I watched her take it. I assumed she was one of his groupies who wanted a memento. But the more I thought about it, the more I realized I had to get the bottle. On the off chance that someone discovered the powdered eggs and knew about Dillon's allergy, I would be in trouble."

"I never wanted to hurt you either, I swear," he tells Mia who scoffs at him. "Do you know I even broke into your apartment one day while you were out. But it was such a mess I couldn't make heads or tails of it. I don't think I could find anything in there. I tried to tell myself it didn't matter. No one would ever suspect there was egg in the drink. No one even knew Dillon was allergic! But it gnawed at me. I had crazy dreams at night.

"I realized I had to follow her," he continues to tell the rest of us, "hoping she would lead me to the bottle, just in case. Sure enough, one day, I saw her leave the apartment holding it. When she went to the chemistry lab, I knew somehow she'd found out about the egg, so I had to get it back. I waited until she went into the closet, locked the door, grabbed everything I needed, and took off."

"I wasn't suspicious about the drink being contaminated you doofus. I only wanted to figure out the formula," Mia snarls.

"How was I supposed to know that?" he laughs maniacally. "Hold on a second. What made you think Dillon didn't die of natural causes?" he asks.

"I was wondering when he would figure it out," Juliet murmurs.

"I don't think you'll believe me if I tell you," I respond.

"What have I got to lose?" he says.

"I'm a spirit communicator. I talk to dead people."

"So, you held a seance and communicated with Dillon? That's a bunch of hooey. I don't believe that for a second."

"I talk to ghosts."

"Get out!" he snorts. "You're telling me you talked to Dillon's ghost?"

"He appeared to me during the celebration of life and said he was certain he'd been murdered. He threatened to haunt the gym and put it out of business if I didn't investigate his death."

If this weren't so serious I'd laugh at how pale Theo's face got. I'd even say he reminds me of ghost.

"You know when you and your friend showed up at my office asking questions, I knew something was up. I figured it had something to do with locking that girl in the closet. That's when I decided I had to get rid of the bottle."

"Why didn't you throw it in the Colorado River where there'd be no chance of someone finding it?" Wendy asks.

"I was on my way to the river when I got nervous. I just wanted to dump it as quickly as possible so I dumped it in the nearest trash can. Not in a million years did I think anyone would notice it. By the way, thanks for the ridiculous story about ghosts. When the authorities get here I'll tell them you're all nuts. In fact, I'll have you arrested for kidnapping. Your ridiculous ghost story will never hold up. I'll deny everything I just said because you have no proof."

"Think again," Sheriff Mack exclaims as he bursts into the lab followed by several deputies. He holds his phone aloft like it's a trophy he just won. "Ms. Daniel dialed my number a while ago. From what I can tell, she did it while they were running to the science building."

I nod, trying my darndest not to smile because he called me Ms. Daniel. It's the little things!

"I heard everything," he says.

"Me too!" head injury ghost exclaims.

# Chapter 30

"Glenwood Springs loves a party!" I shout over the celebratory music and excited chatter from the crowded gym parking lot. Bob clearly went all out with the grand re-opening.

We were all relieved when he had a change of heart and decided to give it one more chance. When he stopped by to say hello earlier in the party I told him I was convinced his bad luck was behind him. "I hope you're right!" he sighed, not realizing Dillon was next to him nodding.

"We sure do!" Wendy exclaims, saluting me with a watermelon daiquiri.

"Wasn't it just yesterday you were overindulging in peppermint martinis at the Christmas party?" I laugh.

"Don't remind me," she groans, cringing at the recent memory.

"The 4th of July celebration is next weekend!" Juliet announces, toasting us with a brightly colored cocktail. The kind with a tiny umbrella perched on top.

"We're going to the pool party to watch fireworks, right?" I ask.

"Of course!"

"I got a huge popsicle shaped raft that we can sit on during the show!" Juliet says.

"Is it me, or are Erica and Joel looking unusually friendly?" Wendy asks, pointing to the chummy couple sitting on a bench, without an inch of space between them.

"Tell her it's not just her. He's the baby daddy," Dillon whispers in my ear.

"You don't have to whisper," I remind him.

"Oh, that's right," he giggles. "Old habits die hard. Get it? *Die* hard?" he guffaws.

Ghosts are so weird.

"But for reals?"

"For reals," he responds, nodding.

"It's not just you," I tell Wendy. "He's the dad."

"How did you find out?" I ask him.

"I overheard him giving Bob his notice."

"He quit?"

"He sure did. Bob asked him to take over my classes once the gym re-opens, but he said he was moving to Iowa."

"Iowa?"

"To be near Erica's parents," Dillon nods knowingly. "He already has a job at a gym and everything. They thought it would be best to get a fresh start where no one knows them."

"I think that's a wise choice," Juliet responds after I repeat what Dillon said.

"By the way." I smile at him. "It was nice of you to have a conversation with Mia and Erica. I think it gave them some closure."

"Eh, I know I was a jerk when I was alive." He shrugs. "I might as well do something good in the afterlife, right?"

"Hello there, Holly!" Ivan says, strolling toward us, looking as proud as can be.

"Congratulations!" I tell him, pointing to the massive RevitaHydrate banner, hanging over a large table piled high with his colorful sports drink. A growing crowd of partygoers gathers, their hands outstretched, begging for sample bottles while his team hands them out as fast as they can.

"I came up with that name," Dillon boasts. "I can't believe he used it, though. That's so cool."

"Phew!" Ivan grins. "Pretty incredible, huh? I knew it would be popular, but this is unbelievable. My phone rings nonstop. Everyone wants it in their stores. I remember when we were worried about having enough buyers. Now I worry about having enough product for all the buyers!"

"So, you've gone national already?" Juliet asks.

"We've gone international! I had to double the size of our warehouse!" he exclaims, excitedly.

"Tell him I'm really proud of him," Dillon says.

"You must know how proud Dillon is, right?" I tell him.

"You feel it too?" he says, with a gleam in his eye. "It's like he's here with us, enjoying all the hoopla."

"Oh, he's definitely with us," I assure him.

"Thanks for saying that. I appreciate it. I should go back to the table to help those guys out. They look like they're about to drop," he says before hurrying over to shake hands with his fans and pass out more drinks.

"Ladies." Sheriff Mack nods as he approaches us.

"Good afternoon, Sheriff," Juliet says. "Oh, look, there's someone we know!" She points in the distance.

"Where?" Wendy asks, as Juliet drags her away leaving me alone with the Sheriff where we spend several moments in awkward silence. When we both start to talk at once I stop first, giggling nervously while the Sheriff shifts his feet.

"I'm not big on apologies," he mumbles before taking a deep breath. "But in this case, I owe you a very big apology. I was out of line to talk to you the way I did and I'm sorry. It won't happen again."

"I appreciate the apology Sheriff. By the way, did you tell Theo, Dillon said he had no intention of leaving him?"

"I did," he laughs. "I'm not sure he believed me though."

"Maybe he didn't want to believe you."

"Hey, so, the department is having a community-wide barbecue on July 4th. You ladies should come."

"That sounds nice," I tell him.

"Okay, well, see you later," he says.

"See you later."

"You guys would make a cute couple," Dillon whispers in my ear.

"Oh, stop it!" I scowl, mostly so he doesn't see me smile.

"So, this is it, huh?" he says. "Time for me to live up to my end of our agreement."

"You're going now?" I ask.

"I thought I'd squeeze in a few more tricks for giggles, but then I'll go," he assures me. "Nothing too serious!" he laughs when I glare at him pointedly one last time. "Only a few hijinks to make everyone wonder."

"All right, have fun. But not too much fun!" I waggle my finger at him.

"Thank you very much, Holly Daniel, paranormal private investigator; I appreciate your sticking with me and believing me, even when it looked like I was making things up."

"You're welcome. I'm sorry that you had to be murdered, and that it was someone you thought was a good friend. But I'm glad I could use my gift to discover the truth."

"Catch you on the flip side," he says right before he runs over to the sports drink table, flinging a pile of fliers in the air startling everyone.

# More Books by B I Skinner

**Ghostly Glenwood Mysteries Paranormal Cozy Mysteries**

The Case of the Haunted Hotel

The Case of the Pilfering Poltergeist

The Case of the Poached Peridot

The Case of the Gym Ghost

The Peach Cobbler Caper

The Case of the Haunted Radio Station(pre-order)

**Spooky Shanty Realty Mysteries**

Afterlife in the Attic

The Lifeless Listing(pre-order)

**Marcall's Breakfast Cafe Paranormal Cozy Mysteries**

An Eggscellent Day for Murder

24 Carrot Caper

Daggers and Donuts

Cupcakes and Corpses

A Crime of Cranberry

Peppermints & Pandemonium

Star Spangled Homicide

Blood Curdling Ballots

Sign up for my email list here

https://mailchi.mp/9ebce0da866a/email-signup-list

Visit my website

biskinnerauthor.com

Follow me on Instagram **@biskinnerauthor** Facebook **@biskinnerauthor**

**Cover art by Spellbinding Designs**

www.ingramcontent.com/pod-product-compliance
Lightning Source LLC
Chambersburg PA
CBHW031541150726
47990CB00001B/251